About the Authors

Jonathan and Jonas both grew up in Northern Virginia. They have been working with children for several years. Jonathan is a third-grade teacher and has taught in Myanmar, the US, and the UK. Jonas worked and volunteered at a few development agencies and education NGOs while living in Myanmar and continues that work in Denmark.

Elfis

Jonathan Spees & Jonas Kjaer

Elfis

Olympia Publishers
London

www.olympiapublishers.com
OLYMPIA PAPERBACK EDITION

A CIP catalogue record for this title is
available from the British Library.

ISBN: 978-1-80074-854-5

This is a work of fiction.
Names, characters, places and incidents originate from the writer's
imagination. Any resemblance to actual persons, living or dead, is
purely coincidental.

First Published in 2023

Olympia Publishers
Tallis House
2 Tallis Street
London
EC4Y 0AB

Printed in Great Britain

Dedication

To my son, Dominic, may you find endless joy in the pursuit of your dreams and passions, and to Lily, your support made this all possible.

Acknowledgements

We would like to thank everyone that patiently read the several versions of Elfis, and gave two clueless authors their thoughts, notes, and patience. They all helped to make this book its best possible version. And to everyone who reads this book after publication, we would like to thank you for your time and hope you enjoy reading this book as much as we enjoyed writing it!

Prologue

"Elfis! I'm not going to ask you again, wash your hands and get to the table, your dinner is getting warm, and I'm not making anything else for you if this goes off!" Holly yelled at her son, who unsurprisingly didn't hear a word she said. He was distracted once again by the show he was watching, Elvis in Concert, for what must have been the hundredth time. He watched this concert, or rather, some Elvis concert regularly, and while he was watching the rest of the world may not have existed for all he was concerned. "ELFIS!!!" Elfis jerked out of his reverie…

"Coming, Mom," he cried out as he scampered in to eat his food.

Chapter 1

The North Pole

A lot of what humans know about elves and the North Pole is surprisingly accurate, which is especially impressive when one considers that no human has ever set foot in the North Pole. Or at least the North Pole that humans are familiar with. It is a very happy place, and there is snow and ice as far as the eye can see. The temperature is always below freezing, which is how elves prefer it of course, and it snows three hundred and sixty-one days a year. There are thousands of snowmen running around, after all, elves love making snowmen, and with their special brand of magic, each snowman made becomes a living, breathing part of the North Pole. "Oh, I'm sorry, I haven't introduced myself, I'm Mrs. Claus and I'm delighted to share this story with you."

The population of the North Pole is officially a state secret, but there are a lot of elves, otherwise, the huge job of making enough toys for every child in the world could never be accomplished. Elves are happy beings, infectiously so, and they are at their happiest when making toys. That is why they love Christmas. They love the singing, the decorations, the food, the holiday cheer, and especially, all the candy canes and sugary icing cookies that Santa isn't able to finish on his own. When elves aren't busy making toys, their favorite leisure time activity is having snowball fights.

Not everything humans know about elves and elf culture is entirely accurate however. Human movies and tv shows would have you believe that Christmas is all they care about. They do love Christmas, but it's not all elves love. Elves have other hobbies and interests and when they clock out at five p.m. they pursue those interests and forget about toy making for the night. Santa doesn't expect elves to make toys twenty-four hours a day, and even if they wanted to (and some of them do), he wouldn't let them. There are a few horror stories about elf burnout. In fact, most of the toys that break or malfunction were caused by an overworked elf. Humans don't work twenty-four hours a day and neither do elves.

Another misconception is that elves only make toys. They do of course make toys, but they also make other things. That phone that your dad gives your mom, that shiny car that you hope to get on your sixteenth birthday, elves make those too. It seems like in your movies elves are only ever making wooden horses or model trains, but elves are terrific with technology, and are almost solely responsible for most products you all use to make your lives easier, better, or more fun, so, you're welcome. This fact leads me to another elf, or rather North Pole misconception, one that few humans would suspect and even fewer would believe if they were told. Santa doesn't only leave the North Pole on December 24th. That used to be the only time he left the North Pole to deliver presents, but with the demand for toys and gadgets and cars and anything else you can think of constantly growing, Santa has pretty much a full-time job on his hands. One my husband loves doing to be sure, but it is no longer just one busy night. December 24th is still his busiest, and his favorite day of course, but now he has to make hundreds of deliveries a year. After all, who do you think restocks warehouses, electronics shops, or book-stores?

The last thing that most humans do not know about elves is that they have a fascination with, and love consuming human culture. They love watching human movies, (not the horror ones of course), they read books you write, listen to music that you create, and some of the more adventurous even eat the food you make, (although, you'd never catch me eating sushi personally). And this is important, because it is this very fact that brings us to our protagonist, Elfis. For, every story needs a main character, even an elven story, and we are about to meet ours.

Chapter 2

March of the Penguins

"Oh good, I haven't heard this song in almost two hours" Elfis said as he rolled his eyes at Ginger. "You know, I really don't get why Christmas carols are the only thing that ever gets played over the loudspeaker," he said in his characteristically slow way of speaking. He had recently taken to adding a southern drawl to his speech as well, and Ginger knew exactly what the idea behind this was. As if anyone who knew Elfis would be even slightly confused as to why he had added this affectation. With his gelled and perfectly blond hair, Elfis stood at a towering three feet and four inches, (five with shoes on as he reminded anyone who asked) which made him extraordinarily average for an elf. Elfis was also the only elf who wore clothes under his work clothes. He had long ago replaced his red work jacket with a faux leather one, and underneath his work pants, he was usually wearing his faux leather pants to match his jacket. He was also prone to wearing sunglasses almost all the time when outside (the North Pole is awfully sunny after all), and his shoes were always so well polished, you could see yourself in them.

"Oh jeez, not again," said Elfis's best friend.

Gingersnap, or Ginger to her friends, was a couple of inches shorter than Elfis, but she had a confidence about her that seemed to give her an extra foot. She had dark brown hair that matched her skin, and although there was nothing romantic between the two best friends, Elfis knew how pretty and smart Ginger was.

"And what would you prefer, Elfis, rock music I suppose? Not exactly conducive to a positive toy making environment, is it? Come on, stop whining and hand me that wrench, as soon as we finish this bike we can clock out for the day."

Ginger had heard this complaint from Elfis time and time again, it was almost a daily routine. He was always talking about changing the music in Santa's workshop. Elfis was an anomaly among elves, he hated Christmas music. He was the only elf Ginger had ever met who didn't like the classics, it made no sense. In fact, if elves weren't such accepting, kind creatures, he would have been looked at strangely due to this aberration. Ginger, on the other hand, loved the music played in the factory, like every other elf not named Elfis. Not to mention, Christmas music was statistically proven to motivate elves more than any other type.

"I know, I know," Elfis remarked, "I would just love a little more variety in our daily catalogue, but you're right. Plus, I suppose, people like, Otis Blackwell, Chuck Berry, and the King wouldn't exactly motivate people to get their work done. They'd be too busy dancing, toys wouldn't get made, the whole operation would be in jeopardy." Elfis smirked.

"Yeah, that's why Santa doesn't want rock music in the factory." Ginger laughed, as she tightened the screw of the back wheel to the beautiful bike that they (generous, as

Ginger was the true craftsman) had been making for the last hour or so. "There, all done, not a bad day. Three bikes, four Lego sets, a couple of pairs of soccer cleats, and a complete set of Star Wars action figures." Ginger satisfyingly ran down their list of toys for the day and gave Elfis a high five.

"Awesome! Let's get out of here before you decide to start work on anything else," Elfis teased his best friend as they cleaned up their area and prepared to clock out for the evening.

Ginger took great pride in her toy making abilities. She was widely regarded as the best young toy maker in Santa's Workshop; her work was often remarked upon by the full-time employees because of how good it was. Elfis and Ginger, at only fourteen years old, were still just part-time workers at the toy shop, as Santa had very strict rules about how many hours younger elves could work, if they wanted to work at all. Elves are not required to work, just like humans, however, it's difficult to make money if you're not working, but Santa doesn't force elves to make toys. It helps that most elves love making toys, and they are paid fifteen candy canes an hour to do so, more than a decent wage for any elf. Until an elf turns eighteen, they can only work fifteen hours a week, but Ginger could not wait until she could become a full-time employee. There was no doubt that she would become one of the best toymakers the factory had ever seen.

"You up for a snowball fight before going home?" Elfis asked Ginger as they left the factory. "Look at all this fresh powder, perfect conditions for a fight." When Ginger didn't answer him, he looked over to see what was wrong. "Ummm, Ginger?"

She was no longer walking next to him; she had vanished quicker than hot chocolate with a candy cane straw on Christmas morning.

"Ginger!" Elfis yelled out, confused. As he turned the other way, he saw a perfectly round projectile heading directly towards him. "Oh puffin," he said before being hit right between the eyes with a ball of powder.

"You're dead!" Elfis yelled out with a smile as wide as his cheeks would allow, in the direction the snowball had come from. He bent down and started building his arsenal up while looking for a safe place to duck behind. About twenty feet to his right, he saw the remains of a snow fort built a few days earlier. "Perfect." Elfis crouched down, picked up his snowballs, and quickly crawled to the barrier. Elfis got to the barrier just in time as snowballs bombarded his fort, he was protected from the barrage of ammunition but was pinned down. Hoping to provide a respite from the endless snowballs being launched from his best friend, Elfis leapt up and fired five snowballs in the general direction of Ginger.

"Ow!" he heard in the distance and knew one of his snowballs had found the target. With Ginger's location now identified, Elfis worked on closing the distance between them without providing her with a target. Elfis saw a particularly large snowman a few yards to his right. He threw one more snowball as a distraction and dove behind the snowman, who looked down at him curiously. Elfis made a shushing gesture up at the larger than average snowman.

"Stay behind me," the snowman said, not picking up on Elfis frantically trying to get him to be quiet. "I'm the best snowman ever, no one has ever seen such a big, strong, powerful snowman, I've done more for elves than any snowman ever built before me." Elfis stood up and put his hand over the snowman's mouth to keep him quiet.

All of a sudden, the endless stream of snowballs stopped. Elfis knew his cunning enemy was refortifying her position, and possibly changing her plan of attack. Elfis used this time to find a new, quieter snowman, and then he started to dig rapidly. He had decided to use this new snowman as cover while digging an underground bunker. He would lull Ginger into a false sense of security, use the bunker as his base, and then flank her from the left, leaving her defenceless and walking home sopping wet and cold. Elfis dug out his bunker and hid a number of snowballs just in case he needed to come back for more ammo. Then, he silently slipped out from behind his snowman fort and crawled out into the open. The terrain was quiet, he looked everywhere for some sign of Ginger, but couldn't find any. He took off his red hat and put it down standing straight up and rolled away from it. A classic distraction manoeuvre to draw her gaze from his actual position.

Elfis continued forward making as little noise as possible, he was a little disturbed by the lack of sound coming from his enemy, he couldn't decide what to make of this sudden ceasefire. He took a risk and got up into a crouch position so as not to have to lie in the snow, as without his hat he was starting to get a little cold and wanted to minimize his contact with the fresh powder. As he continued to try to pinpoint where exactly Ginger had moved to, he was struck on the side of his face by another snowball and he leapt into action. Elfis charged off in that direction throwing caution to the wind. As he was running, he saw a small mound with the tip of a hat just barely sticking out above the snow.

"Got you," he said triumphantly to himself.

Elfis put on even more speed and dove forward with a snowball in hand. As he passed the barrier that Ginger had made. he cocked back his right arm and launched a snowball as hard as he could directly at… nothing. Ginger had tricked him, she had used the same distraction ploy he had, her hat was sitting on a snowman's head and she was nowhere to be found. As Elfis hit the ground, he rolled into a defensive position looking every which way at once, and he heard a bunch of growling coming from the other direction. As he turned to face the direction of the growls, he knew he had been beaten. Elfis opened his mouth to scream as a dozen or so emperor penguins waddled their way towards him, but before he could, a snowball flew over the head of the first penguin and hit him in his mouth, filling it with snow. While Elfis had been busy building his arsenal, Ginger followed the old adage of strength in numbers and recruited the penguins. Before he could recover, another one hit him in his forehead, and then a third came down with expert precision and landed directly on his head. As the penguins closed the distance they broke out and circled Elfis and he finally saw Ginger marshalling her army of fighter penguins.

"Surrender!" Ginger demanded as Elfis was forced to drop his snowball harmlessly to the ground.

"Using penguins to achieve your goal, that's low Ginger," Elfis said good-naturedly, "but, I'll be ready for them next time." He laughed. Elfis took a knee and conceded defeat to Ginger.

"Oh yeah," Ginger smugly replied as she rubbed one of the penguin's heads before it ran off to join the others. "Now, let's get home before we both freeze out here. I for one need an IV of hot chocolate, stat. Don't forget your hat!"

Elfis grabbed his hat and hurried to catch up to Ginger. Out of breath and freezing, the two walked home together. Their families had been next door neighbors since before they were born and they had been best friends since they could talk.

"You want to come over for dinner?" Elfis asked Ginger. "We're having fruitcake."

"I can't tonight, eating with my parents, but do you want to play Elfcraft later?" Ginger asked.

"Aww, I wish, but I've got to practice, I feel like I haven't played my guitar in ages."

Ginger rolled her eyes at this remark. "How's your song coming anyway?" she asked Elfis.

"Not great," Elfis replied. "I can play almost every song Elvis ever wrote, but I can't for the life of me write my own. Every time I try, I just end up with a worse version of one of Elvis's songs. It would help if I didn't have to figure everything out on my own, but no one in my family will ever help me, that's for sure," Elfis finished sadly.

"Are your parents ever going to let you take lessons?" Ginger asked her friend sympathetically

"I don't know," Elfis said, a bit dejectedly. "I keep asking them, but they want me to focus on toy making, they want me to be as good as you and my brother are. I keep telling them you're the best toy maker and I'll never be as good as you, but they keep bringing it up."

"Stop it, Elfis, you are good at making toys, you just get a bit too distracted," Ginger said, embarrassed, she knew she was an exceptional toymaker but she was also a very modest and kind girl. "That's why we work so well together!"

Elfis nudged Ginger on the shoulder. ''Yeah right," he said, "You're the best Ginger, even Santa is impressed by your work. You're going to end up running the factory one day, mark my words!"

Ginger blushed and brushed off the compliment. As she did, Elfis's pet arctic fox came bounding out of the house excitedly. "King!" Ginger yelled and ran to meet the animal. "Hi cutie!" King jumped into Ginger's arms and barked contentedly. Elfis reached over and gave the fox a pet behind the ears.

"Hey King, did you have a good day?" Elfis asked the fox. Elves are of course notoriously good with animals; what might prove a dangerous pet to a human is an elf's best friend. No one is quite sure why this is, it's possible that animals can sense an elf's kind nature and therefore do not feel threatened by the creatures. Another possible explanation is that after centuries of living peacefully with elves, the self-preservation instincts that animals feel around humans have disappeared entirely. An elf mistreating an animal would never happen, the very idea of this is laughable. Even polar bears present no danger to elves, although they do prefer to stick to themselves for the most part.

Naturally, this means elves are vegetarians (as long as it's sugar-coated of course), so it's a good thing that the vegetation that grows in the North Pole is lush, delicious, and plentiful. Elves have all sorts of different types of fruits that humans wouldn't believe. While they don't eat meat, they have the snuffle pod which tastes exactly like chicken when it's picked straight from the vine. This isn't the only type of plant that elves grow. They have fruits that taste like bacon, vegetables that taste like steak, they even have a nut that tastes like salmon! So while elves would never dare to eat an animal, they are not missing out on anything.

Ginger put King down and he ran around the two of them yipping and nipping at their heels. "OK boy, I'm happy to see you too, was Twinkle nice to you today?"

As Elfis asked this question Twinkle herself walked slowly out of the house. She was only three and still walked with both arms out so as not to fall over. Twinkle loved her brother, and Ginger as well, so she was always ecstatic to see them come home from work, and as soon as she saw King bolt out the door, her face lit up like a Christmas tree. She picked her way carefully over the snow trying her hardest not to fall and let out a loud, high-pitched cry, "ELFIS!" She picked up her pace and managed to get all the way to Elfis without tumbling.

Elfis pretended to ignore Twinkle until she was right in front of him and then he scooped her up in a big bear hug while she laughed. "Hey munchkin, did you have a good day?"

Ginger, who also couldn't resist the adorable girl now on her best friend's shoulders, reached up under her arms and tickled her. She gave out a cry of delight and clapped her hands, begging Ginger to stop. "What did you do all day Twinkle?" Ginger asked her, as Twinkle squirmed off of

Elfis's arms in order to be embraced in another bear hug from her other best friend.

"Nothing," she said innocently to Ginger. Adorable as she was, Ginger was not fooled, Twinkle was always causing some sort of trouble, the fact that she was too cute to punish didn't help at all either.

"Yeah right." Elfis laughed at his sister, as he made a mental note to check his room to make sure nothing had been tampered with or was missing. "Anyways," Elfis said to Ginger, "I'll text you a little later," he said to his best friend.

"See you tomorrow, E." Ginger put Twinkle down, and the two slapped hands. Ginger left to go to her house, while Elfis escorted his baby sister and pet fox inside.

Chapter 3

Dinner

As Elfis walked into his house the delicious smell of fruitcake greeted him and his stomach let out a loud growl.

"Elfis," his mother called to him, "about time, quickly get changed, dinner is almost ready." Elfis took his shoes off and went up to his room. He opened his door, tapping the Graceland nameplate he had hung up once for luck, and looked in at his homage to "the greatest rock star that ever lived." He had a huge poster of the King in his famous white suit hanging above his bed, his guitar was set properly on its stand (Twinkle knew not to mess with the guitar), a replica of Elvis's white glitter cape and suit that Ginger helped him make hung on his closet door, waiting for him to wear it, and his vintage record player sat on his desk with the "Frozen" soundtrack resting and ready to play. Elfis shook his head, removed his sister's record, and replaced it with "Elvis, Live from Memphis", and quickly changed out of his soaking wet work clothes, and ran downstairs to eat the delicious dinner his mom had made after a long day.

As Elfis took his customary seat at his kitchen table, his entire family looked at him a touch impatiently. "About time," Twinkle said and everyone at the table chuckled.

"Yeah, what took you so long E?" Frost asked his younger brother. Frost was four years older than Elfis and anyone that had ever met him loved him. Frost was tall for an elf, and had jet black hair that effortlessly framed his almost too good-looking face. He was also an incredible athlete, was the best student when he was in high school, and was one of Santa's most reliable elves already, even at such a young age. Sometimes Elfis resented living in his brother's shadow. But Frost was also incredibly kind and friendly. Elfis knew that there was nothing Frost wouldn't do for him, or anyone, and Elfis could rely on him for anything.

"Sorry guys, I got caught up in an epic battle of good vs evil on my way home."

"Well, I hope at least good triumphed!" his mother said, winking at her son. Holly had a very easy way about her. Holly was as short as Frost was tall, but she was always in a good mood. She was also a very calm woman, which came in handy whenever Elfis and his father got into arguments, which happened more frequently than she cared to admit.

"Unfortunately, not, I was undone by a penguin maneuver," Elfis said with a smile. He reached over and took a large portion of the delicious meal his parents had prepared. "How was work, Dad? Where were you today?"

His father looked over at Elfis. Jack was a handsome man, with the same black hair his oldest son had. He was also very well regarded by his colleagues and peers, he was an incredible toymaker, and as a result was almost exclusively put in the most difficult sectors of the factory. He was also a very serious man, and could be quite intimidating with his deep voice and piercing gaze. "I was working on cars today, they're in the lower level of the workshop" Jack explained. "We managed to perfect the auto-drive feature I think, so we are revolutionizing how humans are going to drive. If we can get this on all cars, we will decrease traffic accidents by eighty-five percent, not to mention the immediate positive impact this will have on the planet. Gasoline usage will plummet!" his father said. "Even the big guy stopped in to look at our work, he said he couldn't believe the progress we had made in so little time!"

"You saw Santa!" Twinkle interjected. Jack smiled, while interactions with Santa happened frequently, his daughter still couldn't believe it every time a story involved him.

"I sure did my sweet." He laughed and rubbed her head affectionately. Twinkle could always make Jack smile, and when he did his face left that stern, serious demeanor behind. "What about you Elfis, how did you do today?"

"We had a good day," Elfis told his father. "Ginger and I got our entire list done and then some! I made a small mistake," Elfis admitted sheepishly, "on one of the bikes we were working on, I accidentally forgot to put on a three-speed gear control system and put on a seven instead, but she caught it and fixed it before it even had a chance to go to final inspection!"

"That Ginger is a marvel," his mother said. "Is there a toy out there she can't make?"

"If there is, it hasn't been discovered in the North Pole," Jack fondly responded. Elfis regretted starting this conversation at once. Every time Jack talked about Ginger, it seemed like he wanted her as a daughter more than he wanted Elfis as a son. Elfis couldn't help but think his father was disappointed in him for not being as good a toymaker as his best friend or brother. Jack turned serious again in the blink of an eye. "You need to be careful when you're working Elfis, some mistakes have larger consequences than just delivering a bike with too many gears. You can't lose focus in the workshop, that's how humans get hurt," Jack finished sternly.

Elfis looked down at his plate. "Yeah, yeah. I'm aware," he said. "It's not like you've never made a mistake," he finished under his breath.

Jack glared at his son, but before he could fire off a response, Holly spoke up, instantly defusing the situation. "I seem to remember a certain elf not putting hair on a Cinderella doll because he was distracted talking to his future wife one day too." Holly laughed. "That's what the final inspection elves are there for after all, it's not such a big deal, Jack."

Jack looked as if he wanted to continue the conversation, but at a glance from his wife, he thought better of it. The family continued to eat the delicious meal and chat, but all the while, Elfis was a ball of nerves. So far tonight, conversation with his father had not been as friendly as he was hoping for. He was getting ready to ask Jack once again for guitar lessons, and he wanted his father in the best mood possible. The few times Elfis had brought up this subject his father always seemed to get more upset than was proportionally acceptable. Elfis had always had a bit of a contentious relationship with his father. He wished to himself yet again that he was as good a toymaker as his brother, maybe that would help his case. Every time the subject of music was broached, Jack inexplicably got angry and refused to discuss it for any longer than the time it took to end the conversation.

"Dad?" Elfis asked, trying not to let his trepidation show, "I've got something to ask you."

"Go ahead," his father said sternly, and Elfis knew, even before he asked, how this conversation was going to go, but he had to try, he told himself.

"Well, I think as a high school student, I have proven myself to be responsible and ready to take on new challenges. So, sir, I was wondering if maybe I could start taking guitar lessons soon, like in the next couple of weeks? I'll pay for them as well; it won't cost you a candy cane," Elfis quickly blurted out in an effort to make his case. "Please Dad!"

Jack looked down at his son and didn't say anything for an entire minute. "You've demonstrated how responsible you are?" Jack skeptically asked his son. "Wasn't it just a few minutes ago you were telling me about how you made a mistake while you were building a bike?"

"Well, yeah, but—" Elfis tried to interject.

"And just last week, didn't we get a call from Mr. Blizzard about how you not only forgot to turn in your homework, but also failed a test?" Jack asked his son rhetorically. Elfis sat in silence, fuming, while his father continued. "These don't strike me as the actions of a responsible, mature, high schooler. Rather, they strike me as the work of a lazy, distracted, immature child."

Elfis wanted to defend himself, but he was worried that if he spoke, he would say something he couldn't take back.

"You have proven to me with your actions, several times, that you wouldn't be able to properly handle guitar lessons on top of work and school. You spend far too much time with that guitar upstairs as it is, guitar lessons are the last thing you need," Jack finished, and his tone left no room for any further discussion.

The family was silent. Frost wanted to come to his brother's defense, as he always hated when Elfis fought with his father, but in Jack's current mood, anything Frost said would have probably made it worse rather than helped.

Elfis continued to look down at his plate. "Can I be excused?" he quietly asked his mom.

"Don't you want some dessert?" his mother asked.

"I'm not hungry," Elfis responded. Holly glared at her husband, and before she could excuse Elfis he was already taking his plate over to the sink. The family heard Elfis's heavy footsteps go all the way up the stairs and into his room, followed by the slamming of his door.

Chapter 4

The Scavenger Hunt

The next day, Elfis walked angrily into his classroom, threw his bag on the ground, and dropped into his seat. Ginger looked over at him sympathetically.

"What's up E?" she asked, concerned. "I haven't seen you this upset since we lost the hockey championship to the south pole elves."

"I don't want to talk about it," Elfis scoffed back, ignoring the hurt look that crossed Ginger's face. He reached into his bag and got out his notebook and pencil. He noticed the pencil needed sharpening, and sulking while he did it, stood up and marched to the front of the room. As he was sharpening his pencil Kris came through the door. Elfis tried to shrink away from him to avoid his notice. Ever since they had been put in the same class, Kris seemed to take any opportunity he could to pick on Elfis. Kris saw Elfis trying to avoid him and made sure to hit him with his shoulder on his way to his seat, breaking the freshly sharpened pencil in the process.

"Just leave me alone for once, Kris!" Elfis remarked angrily. Kris stepped back, eyes agape. Usually Elfis did his best to ignore the bullying, as he figured if he ignored Kris, eventually he would get bored and leave him alone, but Elfis was feeling confrontational today and was in no mood to ignore Kris.

"What did you just say?" Kris said with a smirk, overjoyed at the opportunity for further conflict with Elfis.

"Just stop Kris, Mr. Blizzard will be here soon, and anyway, no one is impressed with you being a jerk all the time." Elfis hadn't seen Ginger come up behind him, but what she said seemed to have worked. Ginger was one of the few elves able to get Kris to behave in a halfway nice manner.

"You're lucky your girlfriend is here to protect you, wimp," Kris said and walked to his seat.

"I don't need you to protect me Ginger," Elfis said, still sulking.

"You're welcome," Ginger said. "You know E, whatever has you in such a bad mood, it isn't my fault. Maybe you want to consider taking your anger out on someone else," she finished.

Elfis glared at her, and then took a deep breath. "You're right, Ginger, I'm sorry, I just had a bad night, thank you. Kris is such a jerk!"

"He is," she agreed, "but he's obviously not why you're so upset, what's going on?"

"My dad and I got into it again last night. I asked him about guitar lessons and he blew up at me for no reason. Why won't he let me play?" Elfis said, with a hint of a tear in his eye.

Ginger sat silently. This was not the first time that Elfis and his father had gotten into an argument about guitar lessons. Ginger knew how important this was to Elfis, but his father was adamant that Elfis focus on his toy-making and his schoolwork.

"I'm sorry E." She didn't know what else to say; she obviously wanted her friend to be happy, but she understood Elfis's dad's side of the argument as well. Elfis was her best friend, but he wasn't the best toymaker around, in fact, she could admit it to herself, without her help he probably would've been demoted to floor floater, a position that consisted of going from station to station to see if anyone needed an extra hand or help. It was more busy work than anything else. On top of that he was falling behind in his schoolwork. He had never been a straight A student but this last year he had started to struggle even more than usual. She was worried about him, and knew why his dad didn't want him spending time playing the guitar and imitating Elvis every chance he got. She knew it was difficult for him at home too, as his brother was basically the model elf.

As Ginger was trying to figure out what to say next, the teacher came in and all talking stopped.

"Good morning, Mr. Blizzard," the class said in unison.

"Good morning boys and girls, I hope you all came in ready to learn today," Mr. Blizzard cheerfully greeted them. Everyone loved Mr. Blizzard. He was tall for an elf and had a deep, soothing voice. He was particularly good at connecting with his students and getting them to really embrace learning. "We've got an exciting day planned. First, we are going to discuss the history of the North Pole. Then we'll go on a scavenger hunt where you'll have to search the school to find replicas of all of the materials Santa first used to build his factory three thousand years ago. Then, you all will get a chance in groups to try and make a model of the toy factory using the parts you find, and will get to present it to the class!" Mr. Blizzard finished excitedly. "And a quick reminder before we get started, remember that the talent show is ten days from today, you have a week to submit what you will be doing and get it approved. First prize is a trip to Iceland in Santa's sleigh and one hundred candy canes."

Elfis perked up when he heard about the morning Mr. Blizzard had planned. It was true, he wasn't the best student, however he did like school and tried his best, when he wasn't daydreaming. Not to mention, this sounded like a blast.

"I'm going to put you in groups of three. Once I do, I want you to sit as a group, then after we discuss the history, the remainder of the morning's time will be yours to try and complete the assignment!" Mr. Blizzard said with a smile.

Elfis listened for his name as Mr. Blizzard read out the groups for the assignment. He was elated when he heard that Mr. Blizzard had paired him with Ginger, but of course, to go along with his bad night, his enthusiasm waned when he heard that Kris was going to be the final member of their group. Elfis let out a sigh and looked at Ginger. She shrugged at him and gave him a wink. All things considered this wasn't too bad, he thought. Yeah, he was with Kris, but he was also with Ginger, and besides, Kris did seem to take his schoolwork seriously.

The three of them moved together and as they sat down Kris "accidentally" kicked Elfis in the shin with a smirk. Elfis glared at him, but couldn't retaliate as Mr. Blizzard had just started his lecture on the history of the North Pole.

Elfis tried to listen, he always tried to behave in class, but before long his thoughts started to drift. He thought about his argument with his dad. Why wouldn't he let him at least try guitar lessons? Elfis had been playing for years, he had even gotten pretty good just on his own. But he didn't want to be pretty good, he wanted to be great. He wanted to be as good a guitar player as Ginger was a toymaker. He wanted to be the best! His dad had a point, Elfis begrudgingly admitted to himself, he knew he had trouble both at work and at school. However, he tried his best, and his dad also didn't seem to have the same restrictions on other after school activities. After all, Elfis had played ice hockey until recently. That was a huge time commitment, and his dad was happy to let him play. He only quit because he had wanted to focus on his music. Something about guitar lessons always made his dad upset, and he couldn't for the life of him figure out what it was. Maybe he would ask Frost when he got home, maybe Frost would have some insight as to why his dad always…

"Elfis, earth to Elfis," Mr. Blizzard said, bringing Elfis out of his own head and back to class. The students chuckled as Elfis jerked up and looked around confused.

"Sorry, Mr. Blizzard," Elfis said, embarrassed.

"That's fine, Elfis," Mr. Blizzard replied, a touch impatiently, "but could you please tell us all when the first reindeer came to the North Pole?"

Elfis looked around at a total loss. He hadn't been paying attention at all, he had completely missed Mr. Blizzard's lecture. "I'm sorry Mr. Blizzard, I don't know."

Mr. Blizzard let out a deep sigh, "please try and pay attention Elfis. We have a quiz on this information soon, you'll need to know this stuff."

"I will, sorry again," said Elfis.

Mr. Blizzard nodded at him and continued his lecture,

Elfis promised himself he was going to pay attention, no more distractions, he really did need to do well on their next quiz. For the remainder of the lecture Elfis was all ears, and participated when Mr. Blizzard asked the class questions.

Mr. Blizzard brought his lecture to a close and then handed out the list of things that the kids had to find for their scavenger hunt. He gave the list to Ginger, and Elfis and Kris immediately crowded around her, excited and curious to learn what it was they had to find for their factory. On the list there were sixteen items that needed to be found, and a list of rules, the main one being that they weren't allowed to disrupt any other classrooms while they were looking around the school.

"Cool, this should be fun," Kris said animatedly. In his excitement over the assignment it seemed that he had forgotten to be mean to Elfis. "Where do you think we should start looking?"

"What if we go to the cafeteria first?" Elfis suggested. "There's so much stuff there, I bet we can find a couple of items on this list."

"Yeah right," Kris replied. "Why would anything be hidden in the cafeteria? That's where we eat duh, not very hygienic to have a bunch of scavenger hunt items hidden there. That was a stupid idea."

Kris hadn't forgotten about being mean to Elfis after all.

"Kris, stop it!" Ginger said firmly. ''If you can't listen to Elfis and respect his ideas then I'm going to tell Mr. Blizzard and you'll be working alone. We all want to win this hunt. Can't you just be nice for one day?"

Kris looked at the floor, hurt, and was he maybe a little

ashamed too? "Fine, let's just go, we'll check the cafeteria first, then we'll go to rooms that make more sense."

Ginger looked as if she was going to scold Kris again, but Elfis nudged her arm, "forget it," he said quietly, "let's just go." The two of them gathered the list and headed towards the door, with Kris coming slowly behind them.

The group walked off to the cafeteria, as no running was one of the scavenger hunt rules. Ginger and Elfis were talking animatedly about the assignment, and how they were going to build their factory, while Kris watched them from a few feet back, not saying anything.

When they got to the cafeteria they saw one other group, so apparently they weren't the only ones who had had this idea. Elfis and Ginger lowered their voices to just above a whisper, as they didn't want the other group taking their suggestions.

"You guys go check the closet in the back, I'll look over by the tables," Kris said a bit morosely.

"Okay," the two of them said in unison and went to the back to look.

"Wow, do you think I hurt his feelings?" Ginger asked Elfis quietly. "Kris is never that quiet, he hasn't said much since he made fun of your idea."

"Who cares?" said Elfis. "He never worries about if he's hurt my feelings, if he wants to search on his own then let him, it will be more fun for us anyway."

Ginger hesitated a bit, on the one hand Elfis was right, Kris was always a jerk to him and never seemed to bother with or care how Elfis felt. On the other hand, Ginger couldn't help but feel a little guilty. "Okay," she finally said, "let's see what we can find."

The two of them set about looking through the closet for any of the materials on their list. It was pretty big so they split up. After several minutes of looking the two hadn't found anything they were looking for. They were forced to admit that maybe the cafeteria was a dead end after all. As they left the closet, they found Kris already waiting for them outside. "I found the cardboard box we need. It was under one of the tables."

"Oh nice, Kris!" Ginger said, a touch too cheerfully. "Well done."

Kris nodded and started to walk towards the exit.

"Umm, Kris."

Kris turned back around, a puzzled look on his face.

"I think you owe Elfis an apology. He suggested we look here after all."

"Ginger, stop," Elfis said a bit awkwardly, "just let it go!"

"No," Ginger said. "You had a good idea and Kris made fun of you for it. Kris, if you want to work with us and enjoy the project and this activity, I think you should apologize to Elfis and we can move forward and have a great time the rest of the morning," she finished.

Kris hesitated. He wasn't used to apologizing for his actions, especially when Elfis was involved. "I'm sorry," Kris muttered, just loud enough for Elfis to hear it.

Ginger started to say something, but Elfis spoke over her, "That's okay Kris, let's keep looking."

The rest of the morning passed without any incident. Kris seemed to cheer up a bit, and the three of them actually made a pretty good team. It took about an hour of searching the school to find the rest of the items on the list, and when they got back to the classroom, they found that only two groups had finished ahead of them, giving them a good chance at putting together the factory first!

The three classmates worked on their project quickly and competently. Everyone was getting along for a change and they made fast work of the building. They were sure to keep an eye out for how the other groups were faring as well. As they were putting together the finishing touches, they started to discuss the different parts to their factory and how they were going to present it to the class. The three started exchanging ideas about what the purpose of each of the various rooms were for.

"Obviously we have the factory floor," Ginger said, "and Santa's office."

"Yeah," Kris agreed, "and the canteen for lunch breaks. Also, what if on the second floor we put a break room, a place for the elves to play table hockey, or shuffleboard?"

"That's a good idea," Elfis remarked, excited by how well he and Kris had gotten along all morning. "And, we can put some guitars in the break room too, and a place for the elves to play music!"

Kris started to laugh and Elfis' face dropped. "A guitar in the break room? Yeah right, that's what people want on their break, a bunch of noise and racket when they're trying to relax." He continued to laugh.

"Well I would want to play music on my break," Elfis said defensively. "Playing music always relaxes me."

Kris stopped laughing for a minute, but still with a grin on his face he asked Elfis incredulously, "You play music?"

"He plays the guitar," Ginger cut in. "He's great, Kris, and I don't think a music room is a bad idea."

"No way, Santa would never allow that anyway," Kris said, still chuckling. "It would be way too big of a distraction. Nice try, Smelfis," Kris finished.

Elfis let out a sigh and sat down. "Fine, you present it however you want, Kris." The truce between the two of them was obviously over. "I don't care."

Kris looked ashamed of himself for treating Elfis that way, as after all, they had been getting along all morning, but right at that moment Mr. Blizzard asked them all to return to their original seats and prepare to present their factories. Elfis, Ginger, and Kris got their chance to present and Mr. Blizzard and all the other elves in the class gave them a polite round of applause when they had finished.

"Nice job everyone," Mr. Blizzard said. "You all did great, I loved the additions you put in Santa's workshop, some of them I think would actually increase productivity. It's time for lunch, great job again, and I'll see you all tomorrow."

The class put all their materials away and filed out the door and towards the cafeteria.

"I think we did a great job, E," Ginger said to him. "That was a lot of fun."

"Yeah, it was, I just wish Kris hadn't laughed at my idea. I know a music room wouldn't actually be put in Santa's workshop, but it was just for pretend. Why should it matter if it would distract the elves in real life?"

"I know," Ginger replied, "but don't let it get to you. Up until that point you and Kris were really getting along! He didn't say anything mean or rude all morning, it actually looked like you guys were friends!"

"Yeah right. That'll be the day!" Elfis said and smiled

at her. "It was a fun activity though, even with Kris in our group. I thought it would be terrible, he's such a jerk, I bet even animals can't stand him, but I had a great time. Come on, I'm starving!"

The two picked up their pace and headed for the lunchroom. Before they had gone three steps however, Elfis was nudged softly on his right shoulder. He turned to look at who had bumped him, but before he could, he saw Kris, head down walking quickly with his shoulders slumped. It wasn't the usual forceful nudge Kris usually gave him, and he hadn't stopped to gloat either.

Elfis looked guiltily at Ginger. "Do you think he heard us?"

Ginger met Elfis eyes and nodded, looking equally guilty and ashamed. The two got their lunches and ate, but it was a more subdued lunch than they would have ordinarily had. Neither one of them could ignore how Kris had looked walking to the cafeteria, especially after they all had been getting along so well.

Chapter 5

A Midday Concert

Elfis and Ginger finished their lunch and got ready to go to the factory. It was only a short walk from the school to Santa's workshop, so they put on their coats and boots and left to start their afternoon shift. The two still felt a bit awkward about their encounter with Kris, but as always, on the walk to the workshop Ginger started to get excited about what they were going to build that day.

"I'm itching to get into work, what section do you think they'll put us in today?" Ginger asked him. Elfis wished he could get as excited about work as Ginger always seemed to. He liked making toys, but he could never muster up the same level of enthusiasm as she always had. The only thing that really made him feel as happy as Ginger did about work was when he got to play his guitar.

"Who knows," Elfis replied, "I wouldn't mind being in electronics today, I always like making new X-boxes."

"Yeah," Ginger said with a smirk, "you like testing new X-boxes is more like it."

Elfis smiled back at her. "Well yeah, how else do we know if we've done a good job?"

"I like the electronics quadrant too, but I feel like we get put there a lot," Ginger said curiously. "We had like three electronics shifts to just one sports equipment shift recently."

"Well, think about it," Elfis said to her. "Electronics are the most difficult toy to make that underage elves are allowed to assemble. And, you are the best underage toy maker, so it makes sense that you would be in electronics more than sports equipment, which we all know is where they send the less-talented elves," Elfis finished.

Ginger punched him in the arm kindly. "Shut up," she said. Ginger always hated when people talked about how good she was at making toys, but no one who saw her work could deny that she was the best. She was even better than Frost was when he was her age, and he had once received a personal commendation from Mrs. Claus!

The two arrived at the factory and went to see Mr. Jolly, the workshop foreman, for their assignments. "Hey guys," Mr. Jolly greeted them, "how was school today?"

"Awesome," the two of them blurted out.

"We built a replica workshop, I even wanted to include a music section in the break room!" Elfis finished.

"A music section?" Mr. Jolly laughed. "That would be so much fun!"

"That's what I thought too," Elfis smiled, glad that his idea was appreciated by the foreman, even if Kris thought it was silly.

"So where do you want us today, Mr. Jolly?" Ginger asked eagerly.

"Well," the foreman looked down at them, "how's this for coincidence? You guys made a music break room, and I've got you down for instruments and amplifiers today. Here's your target list and who else you'll be working with!"

Elfis broke into a huge grin, as this was his favorite assignment, and it felt like forever since they had last been set to work in the music room.

"Yes," he exclaimed, "Thanks Mr. Jolly!"

The foreman laughed again and stuck out a fist which Elfis enthusiastically bumped. "Have fun guys."

The two scampered off to their section and for once Elfis was as excited about work as Ginger. "Can I see the list?' Elfis requested. Ginger handed it to him and Elfis let out another exclamation. "Three acoustic guitars, two electric guitars, a drum set, and a couple of amplifiers. Today is going to rock!"

"I love making guitars," Ginger agreed, "and amps are always a bit of a challenge. I could do without the drums though. They're so easy to make."

"For you maybe, I always mess up the tones and levels." Elfis laughed, even this fact couldn't dampen his mood today.

The two arrived at their quadrant and got right to work. Ginger suggested they start with the amplifiers as they would probably take the most time. Elfis reluctantly agreed. He wanted to dive into the guitars, but it was still important to get their work done. Ginger suggested that Elfis put together the frame for the amplifiers while she would handle the electricity and the wiring. They finished the amps and ran a quick check to make sure they had done everything correctly. Of course Ginger's work was perfect, and Elfis had done a nice job too, but he did forget to add the switch that turned the amps on. Ginger chuckled and fixed the oversight.

"OK, drums next," Ginger said, "and then we end the

day with the guitars."

"Fine," Elfis harrumphed.

"Come on, drums are easy, it'll take thirty minutes and then we can really spend some quality time on the axes." She winked at him.

As always, when it came to toy making, Ginger was right. The two finished the drums, and by the time Elfis had finished putting the finishing touches on the snare, Ginger had already gathered all the materials the two would need to finish both the electric and acoustic guitars.

"Frigid," Elfis said, letting his enthusiasm show. "Let's go."

The two got to work on an acoustic guitar. Elfis started right away sanding down and polishing the wood. He shaved the neck of the guitar down and connected it perfectly to the headstock. He punched in and tightened the tuning pegs, and then added the saddle and badge pin. Finally, Elfis grabbed six strings and attached them gently, completing his guitar. He ran his fingers along the strings and stepped back admiring his work. He had no problem admitting that it was a perfect guitar. He looked over at Ginger who was finishing up her first acoustic guitar as well, and she had done a great job too, but Elfis looked at the two newly made guitars and thought that his was just a touch nicer. His was a little sharper and the flare and design of the instrument was sure to light up a kid's face when he or she unwrapped it.

"Nice work!" Ginger said encouragingly, "that could've come straight out of Memphis!"

"Thanks," he said, "yours too. Do you want to make the third acoustic and I'll get started on the first electric?"

"Go for it," Ginger responded, and turned to look at the clock. "We've got another hour, so we may be able to make another drum set too!"

Elfis loved making and playing acoustic guitars, he loved anything music related really, but his favorite thing to make in the world was an electric guitar. He could picture someone using his work to dazzle thousands at an arena, with fans screaming and hanging on every note played. He could even see that rockstar being him, hypnotizing the crowd and giving them the night of their lives.

He set about making the first of two electric guitars. He shaped the body quickly enough, as he had spent so much time learning about and playing his guitar that making them was second nature to him. After the body, he connected the neck and the tuning post. Then he set about really making this guitar his own. He gave the guitar a metallic red body that faded into a glowing green. He bordered the guitar with a silver color that really emphasized the color of the body. Then he added the tone and volume knobs carefully so as not to disturb the still drying paint.

Elfis glanced to his side to see how Ginger was doing. She had finished her second acoustic guitar and had started on the electric one that they needed to complete to hit their desired target for the day.

Elfis turned back to his guitar. Nothing could distract him for long when music was involved. Elfis added the jack input to the guitar and then included the strap post. Finally, finished with the body, Elfis added the tuning post and tuning pegs and the guitar was almost done. All he had to do was add the strings. He looked into the bucket that was full of them. He picked up four and discarded them before he found one that passed his keen eye and harsh judgment, and attached it to the guitar. He repeated this process five more times, sometimes going through ten strings before finding one he found acceptable. He saw Ginger roll her eyes at him but he ignored her. Elfis finished attaching the sixth string and let out a deep breath.

"Well," he said to Ginger, who was also finishing up her electric guitar. "I think I've done it, Ginger, I think I've made the perfect guitar." He joked, "No guitar will ever be as great as this one."

"Yeah yeah," Ginger groaned. Elfis said something similar to this every time he made an electric guitar. "We've got about twenty minutes left, should we try to make a drum set in that time? We should be able to, no problem."

"Give me a minute," Elfis replied. Ginger started to gather up all of the materials they would need for the drum set. As she did this, she didn't notice Elfis grab the guitar cable and plug it into the amp. Elfis turned up the volume on the amp and the guitar and quietly moved back from Ginger so as not to hurt her ears.

"Elfis, can you give me a hand?" Ginger said. When Elfis didn't answer her, she turned around to ask him again. "Elfis?" she asked when she didn't see him. Then she heard it. The unmistakable sound of an electric guitar being strummed gently. She looked back and gave an exasperated sigh as she saw that Elfis had plugged in the guitar and was playing a G chord. "Elfis, you know it works perfectly, you always make great guitars, quit goofing around."

Elfis smiled and winked at Ginger, he then turned his focus back to his guitar, missing the frustration in her face. Elfis played a simple guitar riff and all the other elves working in this quadrant stopped what they were doing and turned to look at the elf that was distracting them. Once he was sure all attention in the room was on him, Elfis broke into a near perfect rendition of "You Ain't Nothing but a Hound Dog." His playing drowned out the Christmas music that usually filled the workshop and he lost himself in the song that the newly made guitar belted out.

Elves love music, though usually it's holly jolly Christmas songs that they love, but it didn't take long for them to give in to the classic rock that Elfis was playing to perfection. Toys were left unfinished as all the elves started to dance and Elfis felt awestruck for a moment. This is what he was born to do. He wanted to be an elf that brought joy and happiness to other people, not in the toys that he made, but in the music that he played. He wanted to captivate a crowd, he wanted a place in history along with Elvis, his idol, and he wanted to be seen as one of the best guitar players and musicians that ever lived, human or elf.

As he started the bridge to get to the second chorus, Mr. Jolly came hustling into the room utterly bewildered by all the noise. "What is going on here?" he yelled in order to be heard over the music and excitement in the room. "Elfis, what in the North Pole do you think you are doing?" The usually jovial face of the workshop foreman was glaring at Elfis in outrage and surprise. Elfis stopped playing mid chord and Mr. Jolly stalked over and pulled the guitar cable from the amplifier, cutting off all noise except for the soft sound of Jingle Bell Rock coming out of the overhead speaker.

"Come with me," Mr. Jolly said abruptly and turned around.

Elfis gulped and looked around at the other elves, all of whom looked like they would rather be anywhere else in the world. Mr. Jolly was the best boss, and none of them had ever seen him in such a state before. Elfis followed him, trying to walk as quietly as possible. He tried to catch Ginger's eye as he left the room but she was the only elf on the floor not watching his tragic march.

Elfis followed Mr. Jolly for what felt like an eternity. Finally they stopped outside of his office. Mr. Jolly opened the door and uttered just one short word. "In." The only times Elfis had been in this office up till now were for positive reasons. Like when Mr. Jolly had congratulated him and Ginger for making more toys in a month than any other elf pair that year. Entering the office with Mr. Jolly frowning and angry was a different proposition entirely.

"Elfis, what on earth were you thinking? Explain yourself."

Elfis looked down at his shoes. After a minute he responded, "I just wanted to test the instrument I made."

"That's not good enough, Elfis, testing your toys is one thing, but disrupting the entire floor for a midday rock concert is another matter entirely, and you know that. Not only did you prevent your colleagues from getting any work done when you decided to grace us all with your talent, but you distracted people in other rooms too. What if an elf had been working underneath a car at the time? You could've caused him or her to jump and the car could've fallen on them. I don't understand what got into you. You and Ginger are always so well behaved at work."

"Ginger had nothing to do with this," Elfis interjected. "It was my idea, she wanted to build another drum set in the time we had left."

"I have no doubt that Ginger wasn't part of your cockamamie rock show. I just don't get why today you had to lose your mind. Make me understand."

Elfis paused for even longer this time. Finally he responded, "I love music Mr. Jolly," he said slowly, "and not just the songs we hear at work. I mean, I do love those," he quickly lied, seeing the expression on Mr. Jolly's face, "but sometimes I need a little change of pace. A different radio station. I love guitars and I love to play, and I had just finished my instrument and I was really proud of it, and I got caught up in the moment. I know it isn't a good excuse, I know I shouldn't have distracted the elves, and the consequences could have been a whole lot worse. I just, one time, wanted to play in front of people. I saw an audience in front of me, and I just wanted to try it. I'm so sorry, Mr. Jolly."

Mr. Jolly saw a tear run down Elfis's face. "I didn't know you were so crazy about music," he said quietly.

Elfis brushed his eye with his hand and looked up. "Yes sir."

"And an Elvis fan, huh?"

"He's the king," Elfis said.

"Okay Elfis. Listen, no one got hurt, no toys were maimed beyond repair, and it's the end of the day, but there is a time and a place for playing music, and I think we can all agree, Santa's workshop when elves are working is not that place, correct?"

"Correct, sir," Elfis responded.

"I don't think we need to continue to discuss and talk about this right? I mean after all, you are NEVER going to do it again, correct?"

"Never! I wouldn't dream of it."

"I'm glad to hear that. We can drop it then, but Elfis, there has to be some consequence for what you did. I'm afraid we're going to take you off instrument duty for the time being. Not permanently, but for the next few shifts, until I say so, you and Ginger will not be working in the music room."

Elfis's face dropped, for a minute he thought he was going to get out of this scot-free. Upon giving his punishment a bit more thought however, he realized that it could have gone a lot worse. He wasn't being suspended, Santa wasn't going to find out, and Mr. Jolly seemed to understand how Elfis felt.

"Okay, thanks Mr. Jolly," Elfis said. "It will never happen again. I'm really sorry."

"That's all right, Elfis, now, go grab Ginger and get out of here, your shift is just about over anyway and it looks as if, despite your rock concert, you guys finished all the items on the list for the day." Elfis stood up and turned to walk out the door. As he opened the door and started to walk out Mr. Jolly stopped him. "Oh, and Elfis…" Elfis turned back around confused.

"Yes, sir."

"Way to rock!" Mr. Jolly said with a shadow of a smile on his face. Elfis turned and left with a grin. It could've been a lot worse, he thought.

Chapter 6

The Fight

Elfis went back to the main floor and gathered his things. He double checked to make sure everything was put away properly (of course it was, Ginger would have done that before she left), and he headed for the door. He couldn't help feeling a bit smug about the interaction he just had. He thought he was really in for it, he had after all distracted the entire floor of the workshop. He had also used one of the newly made toys that was meant for the humans. Something that was strictly not allowed, outside of the usual toy testing. It was a requirement that the toys reach their humans new and in mint condition. But, despite the rules he had broken, he had gotten nothing more than a slap on the wrist. He felt better than he probably should have.

As he exited the workshop, he saw Ginger waiting for him with a grim look on her face. "What happened?" she asked him as he emerged from the workshop.

"You'll never believe it, I didn't get in any trouble, I mean, we aren't going to be on music duty for a while, but that's it. No long-term punishment, he's not even going to tell my dad. And you'll never guess what else? Mr. Jolly likes my playing, he said so right as I was leaving his office!" Elfis said excitedly.

"That's great," Ginger said in a rather higher pitched

voice than she usually spoke with. "I'm glad you aren't getting in trouble. I mean, it was a pretty bad idea to stage a rock concert in the middle of the factory in the middle of the day, but I'm glad everything worked out," Ginger finished. Even in his elated state Elfis couldn't help but notice she was acting a little strange. Something about her tone was definitely off.

"Yeah, I couldn't believe it either. Did you get in any trouble? I'm sure you didn't, after all it was me who was responsible for everything, I'm sure you were okay right?" Elfis asked Ginger.

"Yeah, Mr. Jolly's assistant came to ask me what happened and why we did it, fortunately he believed me when I told him I wasn't responsible. A couple of the other elves on the floor backed me up too. They reassured him that while you were playing your music, I was putting together an extra drum set. So I'm okay, it's too bad we won't be making instruments any time soon, but I guess neither of us are in any trouble."

There was definitely something weird about how Ginger was talking to him. He couldn't quite put his finger on it, but she seemed in a strange mood. Was it possible that maybe she did get in trouble but didn't want to make him feel bad? Or maybe she had just been nervous for him and was relieved to learn that nothing bad had come from the incident.

"Are you sure you're okay?" Elfis asked her.

"Yeah, I'm great, why wouldn't I be?" she replied.

Elfis shrugged. "I don't know, just wondering. Hey, you up for a snowball fight before we get home?"

"Not today, Elfis, I'm pretty tired."

The two walked home in near silence. It was a little uncomfortable, but Elfis had no idea what he could do about it. He wasn't in trouble, so he wasn't sure why Ginger was acting so strange.

"Hey," Elfis said in another attempt to make conversation with Ginger. "Can you believe Mr. Jolly liked my playing? He said it right as I was leaving his office, he told me I rocked before I left."

"You're a great guitar player Elfis," Ginger responded a bit flatly. "I'm not surprised he thought you sounded good."

"Yeah, I was a little surprised," Elfis said. He could see his house up ahead and couldn't wait for King to be let out to meet him. Whatever was eating at Ginger was making this walk very uncomfortable.

As if his words had summoned the fox, his front door opened and the little animal galloped out of his house to meet the two of them. "Hey King!" Elfis said, happy for something to break up the walk. Ginger leaned over and scratched the fox behind his ears as he ran circles around the two of them excitedly.

"Good boy," Ginger said for the first time, sounding like her old self. "Okay E, I'm going to head home, I'll see you at school tomorrow."

"Yeah." Elfis tried to hide the concern and awkwardness in his voice. "See you tomorrow!" The two bumped fists and Ginger walked towards her house. "I wonder what is going on with her?" Elfis asked King. "Very strange," he remarked. King looked up at him blankly and Elfis reached down to pick him up. He happily jumped into Elfis' arms and the two walked home.

His cheerful mood had started to evaporate. Mr Jolly's easy reprimand and his kind words didn't dull his concern about his friend. Ginger had never acted so aloof. He didn't have long to dwell on the issue however, because as soon as he entered his house Twinkle ran into his stomach. Using what he assumed to be all of her force, he had to catch himself before he fell down with the arctic fox in his arms. "Oof, careful munchkin, you're getting bigger," he said happily.

Twinkle's big blue eyes stared right at him. She stuck out her tongue and blew a raspberry at him, and immediately ran away in a fit of laughter. Elfis rolled his eyes. His sister was quite the character, he thought to himself.

Elfis found his mom in their living room with a book open. "Hey Mom. How was work today?"

Elfis's mom closed her book and looked at her son with a smile. "I was busy today, one of the computers in office supplies nearly incinerated itself because someone mixed up the wires in the modem. No harm done though," she continued. "We figured out the glitch and got everything sorted," she said happily. "|These things happen. Your father should be back soon, he had the later shift today, and then we'll have dinner."

"Great, thanks Mom, I'm starving!" Elfis said.

"Where were you assigned today, E?" his mom asked.

Elfis hesitated a moment. He wanted to tell his mom that Mr. Jolly had liked his guitar playing, but doing that would mean he would have to tell her about his bad behavior at work, and that was something he didn't want his parents finding out about. His dad would be pretty upset about his concert. Elfis decided not to tell his mom about the afternoon. "Oh, we were in the music department today," he said. "It was fun," he finished a bit lamely, not wanting to get into the whole story.

"That's great, you love working in the music department. What instruments did you make today?"

Elfis wanted to get out of this conversation as quickly as possible; he regretted starting it in the first place. "A few guitars, some drums, you know, normal stuff." His mom looked like she was going to ask further questions, but before she could, Elfis interrupted, "But, I'm beat mom, we had a big assignment at school this morning and after a long day of work, I'm really tired. I'm going to go up and shower before dad gets home"

"Okay sweetie," his mom said, smiling. "Dinner in about an hour."

"Sounds great, Mom," Elfis replied halfway up the stairs. Elfis walked into Graceland, kicked off his shoes, and flopped onto his bed. He wasn't lying when he told his mom he was tired, today had been a long day. Both physically and emotionally. He picked up his guitar and quietly strummed it. He reflected back on work. It had really felt great playing in front of the other elves. It was hardly Madison Square Garden, but they had all seemed to like his music, and performing in front of them made him feel six feet tall. Elfis put his guitar down and went to take a shower. It had been a pretty good day. He had almost completely forgotten about Ginger's strange behavior.

While Elfis was showering, his dad and Frost both came home. Elfis got out of the shower and thought he could hear slightly elevated voices. He went back into his room and picked up his guitar when Frost knocked on his already open door.

"What's up bro?" Frost said to him. "How was work?" Frost brushed his long dark hair out of his eyes, Elfis noticed that even after a long day of work Frost still looked cool, it was effortless for him.

"Work was good," Elfis responded to his brother's question. "I was in the music department today, I made a rocking guitar, even you couldn't have made it any better."

Frost smiled down at his brother. "I believe you. What else happened?" Elfis looked at his brother, a touch confused. Frost stared at him not unkindly and a little concerned, and then it hit Elfis.

"Oh no," Elfis said and felt his stomach drop into his knees. "Does Dad know?"

"He does," Frost said. "E, what were you thinking?" Frost looked at his little brother with pity in his eyes. "You know how seriously dad takes work, and he already doesn't love how obsessed with music you are."

Elfis felt a lump in his throat. "How did he find out? Mr. Jolly said it would stay between us."

"One of the elves that was working on your floor is a friend of Dad's," Frost explained. "Look kid, it's going to be okay, Mom is downstairs talking to Dad, she'll calm him down a bit, but you need to make sure that Dad understands that this will never happen again. He's not happy, E."

Elfis looked down. "Is he going to ground me?"

"I don't know," Frost answered, "but if he does, you'll be okay, don't worry about it bud, it's not the end of the world. Just go downstairs and face the music." (Elfis didn't appreciate this pun.) "As soon as you do, you'll feel better.

Okay?"

Elfis let out a deep sigh. "Yeah, you're right, I might as well get this over with."

"Hey, on the plus side," Frost said to his younger brother, "Dad's friend said he hadn't heard a better guitar player in years!" Frost smiled. "You'll be fine champ," Frost finished, then he leant over and ruffled his brother's hair before leaving his room. Elfis smiled as his brother went to change for dinner.

Elfis gathered up his courage and went downstairs. Despite it feeling like a year ago after everything that had happened today, it was only last night that Elfis and his dad had gotten into an argument about this very thing. Music and Elfis's love for the guitar always seemed to lead to confrontations between him and his father. And getting in trouble twice in two days for something music related, this was going to be ugly.

"Well," his mom said as he entered the kitchen. "When you were telling me about your day, I guess you forgot about the free concert you gave to half of the workshop huh?" she said sternly. "Elfis, what were you thinking, what got into you?"

"He wasn't thinking, obviously," his father said angrily. "Why else would he have pulled a stunt like this? What is it with you Elfis? We had a discussion about this last night. You want to take guitar lessons, and the way you go about proving to me that you are responsible enough to handle them is to interrupt an afternoon of work to play some fifty-year-old song in the middle of the factory! What do you have to say for yourself?"

Elfis let his dad's tirade wash over him, and when it

came to an end he looked up at his dad. "I'm sorry," he said.

"That's it?" his father replied. "You want me to let you take guitar lessons, and all you can say is you're sorry? I can't believe you haven't been suspended from work for this. I don't know what you must have said to Mr. Jolly, but I intend to find out."

"Well," Elfis started to respond. He could feel his temper rising, and even though he knew now was the time to keep his cool, he couldn't help himself. "It's not as if you were ever going to let me take guitar lessons anyway, is it? I just wanted to feel like a rockstar for once in my life. I wanted to feel like I had a dad who actually let me have fun, and cared about me!" Elfis finished, his voice raised to a shout at this point.

"Elfis, how could you say that?" his mom interjected. "Of course we care about you, we just want what's best for you."

Elfis's dad was not nearly so calm, "You've got a funny way of showing you deserve guitar lessons, don't you?" he said to Elfis, his voice also reaching a crescendo. "Your grades are lousy, you're distracted at school, and the only reason you're not in trouble at work for your shoddy toy making is because you've got Ginger to bail you out anytime you make a mistake."

"Jack!" Holly exclaimed, "Don't say those things."

"It's fine Mom," Elfis said angrily. "It's a relief to finally hear his thoughts out loud. What's the big deal, Dad? Yeah so I played a bit of guitar, I distracted a few elves for a few minutes, did you stop to ask whether or not I had finished my work for the day? Which I had by the way, not that you care. Did you think maybe I aced my project in school today? No, of course not."

Elfis knew he should stop before he said something he would regret, but he was too angry. "Just because all you care about is making toys, doesn't mean that's all I want to do. It's like you're mad because you're not good at anything else. All you can do is make toys, sorry I can do something better than you, sorry it's not what your dream is! What an exciting life you've lived, wake up, make toys, go to bed, how fun!"

Elfis's mom gasped and his dad slammed his hand on the counter. Elfis knew he had gone too far. He looked at his dad in silence, still angry, but now he was nervous as well.

"Go upstairs, and bring me your guitar," Jack said quietly.

"Why?" Elfis asked, his anger evaporating into concern and fear.

"Now," his father said. Elfis was too scared to ask any more questions. He turned around and walked up the stairs. Twinkle was sitting in the hall, clearly eavesdropping, but even she had nothing to say. Their father had never been this mad, and Twinkle, who had a remark for everything, was uncharacteristically silent. Elfis went into his room, grabbed his guitar, and returned to the kitchen. "Give it to me," his father said, in that same, quiet voice. Elfis handed him the guitar, his father took it. "There will be no more guitar in this house," he said. "Not until you can learn how to be a responsible, mature young man. And given that stunt you pulled today, and your attitude tonight, I don't see you getting this guitar back anytime soon. Go to your room."

"Dad," Elfis started, "I'm sorry, I didn't mean it. Please

don't take my guitar away!"

"Tough, maybe now you will realize that your actions have consequences, maybe now you'll focus on your toy making. Maybe you'll be a bit more like Ginger, or your brother, or me. Elves who take pride in their work, who know and realize how important it is that we make those toys, and that everything runs smoothly in the factory. Maybe you'll figure out that billions of humans rely on us, so taking pride in being a good toymaker isn't an insult. Maybe you'll start to pay attention in school for more than one day at a time. But I can tell you one thing you won't be doing, and that's playing this frozen guitar constantly, and neglecting your actual responsibilities. Go to your room," Jack finished. Elfis listened to his father's words, and couldn't help but feel ashamed. His dad was a great toymaker, and that's what most elves aspired to be. He never should have said those things. And now he was looking at who knew how long, if ever, before he would be able to play the guitar again. It was hard to imagine that just two hours ago Elfis had been in a great mood.

Jack and Holly looked at each other. "You know he didn't mean that, Jack, he was just upset."

Jack shook his head. "He did mean it," he contradicted her. "The reason he's not a great toymaker is because he doesn't think making toys is important. He doesn't get better because he doesn't want to get better. We never had this issue with Frost," he finished.

"He's still young, Jack, don't put too much pressure on him." Holly pleaded with her husband. "What if you just had an honest discussion with him, no getting angry, or yelling, just explain all of this to him, tell him about your time as an…"

Jack interrupted her, "That's the last thing he needs, I don't need to put any more ideas into his head than he's already got up there. We've indulged his distracted behavior for years." Jack countered, "We always assumed he'd buckle down when he got older, but he's getting older and he's showing no signs of buckling down. He's in high school now, when Frost was his age, he was already thriving in the factory."

"I know," Holly responded, "but are you sure taking his guitar away is the best move? He loves that guitar."

"That's the problem," Jack said. "I don't want to make him miserable, Holly, but he needs to learn some responsibility. He needs to be held accountable. It's not forever, but I think for now, the best thing for Elfis is some time focusing on school, and work, and not his guitar."

"Maybe you're right," Holly said.

Chapter 7

An Unexpected Friend

The next morning, Elfis woke up feeling sluggish. He dreamt he was on stage with no guitar and a hostile audience was booing him. Looking over to where his guitar should have been, he heaved a sigh, slowly got up and got ready for school. Not wanting to risk a chance encounter with his father, he grabbed a piece of fruit and left the house for school without saying a word to anyone. Elfis was the first one to arrive and as he doodled the rest of the class slowly started to file in. He finally saw Ginger enter the room chatting to Pepper, another friend of hers. Ginger laughed at something Pepper had said as she went to sit at her seat. She put her backpack down and sat in the chair next to Elfis.

"Hey, E," Ginger said, sounding more like her usual self

"Hey," Elfis muttered to her sourly.

"Why so glum, sugar plum?" she joked.

"My dad took my guitar away," Elfis explained. "He found out about work yesterday and we got into another argument. He got mad about my schoolwork. He called me irresponsible and said I'll never be a good toymaker if I don't start taking my work more seriously. Then he took my guitar and wouldn't tell me how long he was going to keep it for. It's so unfair. Mr. Jolly didn't even care about the whole thing!" Elfis finished.

"Oh," Ginger said. "Well E," she hesitated, "he kind of has a point." Elfis looked at her astonished that his best friend wasn't more sympathetic about the whole situation. Ginger continued before Elfis could interrupt, "I mean, it's totally frosty that he took your guitar from you, but music and your guitar do tend to distract you from work and school. Yesterday alone, you stopped work thirty minutes early just so you could play a couple of songs," Ginger finished.

Elfis couldn't believe what he was hearing. "What do you mean," he responded angrily. "We not only finished our entire list yesterday, but we made an additional drum set. We always finish our work. I can't remember the last time we ended a day not having completed our entire list. He had no right to take away my guitar," Elfis finished.

"Well, I finished an extra drum set," Ginger said, almost under her breath. "You quit working to play the guitar," she said.

"What do you mean?" Elfis repeated. This whole morning he couldn't wait to get to school to talk to Ginger, he had been relying on her support, and here she was, telling him not only that she agreed with her dad, but that she did all of their work. "Well we were finished, weren't we?" Elfis asked, in a slightly hostile tone. "Why does it matter if we do an extra drum set at the end of the day? And I helped you with everything else," Elfis said, his voice rising.

"Calm down, E," Ginger responded, "I'm just saying, maybe your dad has a point, you do have a tendency to get distracted and more often than not, music is the reason why."

"Well, what did you mean about the drums then?" Elfis said, his temper still rising. "Like I said, we had finished all of our work, why do we always have to do more than we are supposed to?"

"Nothing, just drop it, Elfis, I'm sorry you had a bad night," Ginger said, trying to deescalate the situation. However, with everything that had happened in the last sixteen hours, Elfis was a little too upset to just let this go.

"I can't believe you're siding with my dad on this one! I figured that as my best friend you would have my back, but I suppose that's asking a little bit too much, huh? Why would you support me? Everyone's always against me. My dad, Kris, you, no one takes my side," Elfis finished.

It was Ginger's turn to be incredulous. "Are you kidding me?"

"What?" Elfis huffed at her.

"I don't support you?" she said.

"Well, it sure seems that way," Elfis responded.

Ginger was furious all of a sudden. "Let me ask you this, Elfis, when you quit working yesterday, did you tell me what you were going to do? Did you let me know that, rather than help me put together a new drum set, you were going to forget all about helping me so you could pretend you were a rockstar in the middle of the workday? Did you think for one second that maybe you causing a severe workplace distraction and potentially ruining countless toys would get me in trouble as we're supposed to be partners? I can tell you the answer to all of those questions, and the answer is no. You didn't think about any of that did you? And then, you leave Mr. Jolly's office yesterday with no consequences while I was left to clean up and defend my lack of participation to the assistant foreman." Elfis was shocked by what he was hearing but he couldn't get a word in edgewise. This must have been what had been bothering Ginger yesterday. At this point the rest of the class had stopped all of their side conversations to witness the unfolding drama of the two best friends arguing for the first time.

Ginger wasn't finished. "And, you have the nerve to say I don't support you? Who is always helping you find time for guitar? Who watches the same Elvis concerts time after time with you when I would rather be watching almost anything? Who helps you with schoolwork so that you can spend more time playing your guitar? And finally, you sit here and say we always finish our work assignments. WE! Elfis, I am the one that always finishes our work assignments. It's because of me that the two of us have such a good reputation with Mr. Jolly, I am always fixing your mistakes and helping you finish toys when we're running out of time. Don't you dare say that I don't support you, Elfis, when it seems to me like you look at me like I'm just your sidekick, someone there to help you on your way to becoming a rockstar!"

"But," Elfis said timidly. "You're the better toymaker," he said as if that made up for every point Ginger had just made. He wondered how long she had been thinking some of these things and he felt lower than he thought possible a mere ten minutes ago.

"That's got nothing to do with it," Ginger interjected. "You're too distracted half the time to even realize you're making a mistake. Who cares if I'm better at making toys?

If you tried half as hard at toy making as you do guitar, I wouldn't have to cover for you almost every day." Ginger finished and took a deep breath, and Elfis could see a tear falling out of her eye. "You don't ever think about other people, including someone who is supposed to be your best friend." The entire room was absolutely silent. You could have heard a snowflake hit the ground.

Ginger stood up out of her chair and gathered her backpack. She walked over to Pepper and asked if they could switch seats for the day. Pepper picked up her backpack and sat next to Elfis, but turned her shoulder to him so he couldn't talk to her. All of this happened just in time, as Mr. Blizzard entered an uncharacteristically subdued class.

Elfis was completely distracted the entire morning. Mr. Blizzard called on him three times in class and all three times he got an answer wrong and had to be reminded what question had just been asked. Mr. Blizzard asked him to stay after class, but for once Elfis hadn't been distracted by music or Elvis, he just couldn't stop thinking about what Ginger had said. Was he really as selfish as she had said he was?

When class ended and they had all been dismissed for lunch, Elfis slowly approached Mr. Blizzard's desk. He couldn't help noticing that Ginger had hurried out of the room and hadn't even looked at him. Mr. Blizzard looked up at Elfis from the paper he was reading. "Not your best morning today was it, Elfis?" he asked rhetorically. "What's going on?"

"Nothing sir, I've just had a rough couple of days. I'm sorry, I'll be more focused from here on out," Elfis reassured his teacher.

"You've said that before, Elfis, but it's really becoming a problem. Your last three test scores have been disappointing, and you need to start improving your grades, or summer school is a real possibility, and I know you don't want that. Do I need to call your father?"

"No," Elfis emphatically responded. "I'll do better Mr. Blizzard, I promise, no more distractions in school."

"Okay, all I ask is that you try Elfis," Mr. Blizzard said kindly. "Go enjoy your lunch!"

Elfis walked to the lunchroom still thinking about everything that had happened over the last day. Between his father taking away his guitar and Ginger yelling at him, he wasn't sure if he'd ever had such a lousy morning. He entered the cafeteria and saw Ginger at a table with a couple of other classmates. There were a few empty seats, but Elfis didn't think he would be welcome at the moment, and he didn't want to upset Ginger any more than he already had. He looked around and was dismayed to see the only table available was Kris's. It was empty. "This day just keeps getting worse," he said to himself.

Elfis walked over to the table and reluctantly asked Kris if he could sit down. Kris with his mouth full made a noise that Elfis assumed meant yes and sat down.

Kris finished chewing his food, and asked, "What are you doing here, Smelfis?"

"Everywhere else was taken," Elfis responded and started to eat his lunch. Kris looked at Elfis waiting for him to say something more, and when he didn't Kris went back to eating his lunch. The two ate in silence for a couple of minutes.

"So," Kris said with a smirk, "Ginger didn't want you sitting with her after this morning I gather?"

"Obviously not," Elfis said angrily. He was tired, upset, and hurt, and was in no mood to deal with Kris being a jerk. "So just make whatever stupid, mean comment you want and then leave me alone to eat my lunch in peace."

Kris hesitated for a moment, thinking about how to respond. Finally he said quietly, "I'm not the only one that says mean and hurtful things, you know?"

Elfis looked up, and realized that Kris wasn't just being a jerk. Elfis had no idea what he was referring to at first, then he remembered what had happened yesterday at lunch. He couldn't believe only twenty-four hours ago things had been going so well and he had been getting along with the school bully. "What do you mean?" Elfis asked even though he already knew.

"I heard what the two of you said about me on the way to lunch yesterday," Kris assured him, "about how even the animals hate me. Real nice of you."

Elfis paused, not knowing how to respond. "Well, in my defense, you are always mean to me, Kris. I'm not sure what I ever did to you, but it seems like every day you make fun of me for something. You called me 'Smelfis' five minutes ago."

Kris hesitated. "You're right," he said. Elfis was shocked, he had expected Kris to be angry at him, or maybe to deny that he was even mean to him in the first place, but he hadn't expected this admission of guilt. Kris continued, "I just… I'm never sure… Forget it."

Elfis had never seen Kris unsure of himself and he wasn't about to let this go. "You just what?" he said.

Kris took a deep breath and Elfis could see he was struggling with something. Everything was upside down today. He and Ginger were arguing, while he was having a normal conversation with Kris. "I don't want to be a jerk, Elfis, it's not as if I wake up in the morning and think 'how can I be mean to Elfis today.'"

Elfis was beyond confused, but had given up trying to make sense of this day. "Then why do you behave the way you do?"

Again, Kris paused. "You guys always just look like you're having so much fun together, and you may have noticed..." Kris stopped and pointed all around the empty table. "I don't exactly have that many friends."

"So, you want to be friends with us?" Elfis asked in genuine shock. "Then why wouldn't you just be nice?"

Kris hesitated. Elfis thought he glanced over at Ginger's table as well. "Forget it," he said again.

Elfis went back to his lunch, he had more than enough to think about. The two sat at the table eating quietly again, Elfis lost in his own thoughts. Kris cleared his throat and Elfis looked at him. "Why did you want a music room in Santa's workshop yesterday?" Kris asked him out of nowhere.

"I just thought it would be fun," Elfis responded.

"Yeah, but you could've said anything, a snowball fight break room, an ice hockey rink, a candy shop, and you went with a music room. I was just wondering why?"

"You don't like music?" Elfis asked Kris accusingly.

"I do, I mean, it's nice to listen to, but for the assignment you could've said anything, and I don't get why you went with a music room."

"I love music," Elfis said defensively. "What does it matter? You laughed and said it was stupid anyway," Elfis responded.

Kris was quiet for a moment. "I'm sorry about that," he said earnestly. "It wasn't cool of me to freeze you like that, I was just kind of surprised that you said it."

Elfis looked at Kris astonished. "Don't worry about it," he said. "It was a bad idea, I proved that yesterday after all."

"Oh yeah," said Kris, "I heard about your rock concert at the factory." He chuckled. "It was cool, people liked it, I heard."

"Not everyone," Elfis said glumly. "And my dad was furious, he took my guitar away from me last night, and we got into a huge fight."

"I guess Ginger wasn't thrilled about it either," Kris said. Elfis listened for any smugness or gloating in Kris's tone, but he couldn't hear any. The two of them were having a real conversation and Kris hadn't been mean or nasty to Elfis once. "She seemed pretty mad this morning."

"Yeah, she was madder than my dad."

"Do you think maybe she was right?" Kris asked Elfis cautiously.

"What do you mean? She's my best friend, we've always worked together and we've never had any issues before this morning." Elfis was getting argumentative. "We do everything together. And she's always loved my music," he finished.

"Look," Kris said, "I don't know too much about you guys and your relationship, but based on what she said this morning, it seems like your friendship is kind of one sided. At least, that's how Ginger sees it sometimes. She's always the one helping you and you don't help her much in return?"

Elfis glared at Kris, but Kris cut him off. "Don't shoot the messenger, Elfis, that's just what it sounded like to me. And it's no secret that Ginger is the smartest kid in class and the best toy maker in the school. Maybe she just wants the same support she gives to you."

Elfis considered a snarky response, but Kris seemed to be making sense, maybe he hadn't been supportive enough of his best friend. She did get him out of trouble and work jams constantly, and helped him with his schoolwork when he was confused, which, he could admit to himself, was often. "Yeah," Elfis said quietly. "Maybe you're right. Hey, thanks Kris," Elfis finished.

"No problem," Kris said, and went back to his lunch.

After a moment Elfis coughed and Kris looked at him.

"What's up?" Kris asked in response to his cough.

"Look, Kris, I'm sorry about what we said yesterday," Elfis answered nervously. "We had all been getting along, and we did a good job on the assignment, and there was no reason for me to say something like that. I'm sorry," Elfis apologized quickly.

Kris stared at him for a moment and waved his hand. "Don't worry about it, I probably deserved that for the way I've treated you for the last several years. Actually, scratch that, I definitely deserved that and probably a lot more if I'm being honest." The two looked at each other and smiled. Kris held out his fist and Elfis bumped it.

"So," Kris started, "what kind of music do you like to listen to the most?"

Elfis chuckled. "Well, I like most kinds of music, but no music holds a candle to rock and roll."

Kris laughed. "I don't think I really know much rock music. I suppose you wouldn't count Jingle Bell Rock, would you?"

"Not exactly," Elfis said lightly, "have you ever heard anything by the King?"

Kris looked at him questioningly.

"Elvis?" Elfis asked incredulously. "The guy I'm named after!" he finished emphatically.

"Sorry," Kris replied a little abashed, "I've never heard of him."

"Well, that's okay, he's my favorite musician, he's the best to ever pick up a guitar if you ask me!" Elfis said with a grin.

"Was it his music you were playing yesterday?"

"Yeah." Elfis laughed. "I played Hound Dog, one of his best songs, and trust me when I say, there are a lot of those to choose from!"

"I'd love to hear some of his music. Maybe you, Ginger, and I could all hang out one day after school and listen to you play the King's greatest hits!" Kris said excitedly.

Elfis's face dropped. "Only If you want to," Kris said quickly. "You guys don't have to hang out with me, I get it." Elfis looked up and saw that Kris was crestfallen.

"No, I'd love to hang out and play some tunes," Elfis reassured Kris. "It's just that I don't know when my dad is going to let me play my guitar again. He was really mad at me last night, and my grades aren't very good this semester. I had almost forgotten about that until just now. Not to mention, Ginger probably won't want to hang out with me either," Elfis finished sadly.

"Oh," Kris said, trying to sympathize with Elfis.

"That's cool, they can't stay mad at you forever, and eventually your dad will give you the guitar back, and when he does, you can rock!" Kris finished sincerely.

"Definitely," Elfis responded with feigned enthusiasm.

"Well, I've got to go," Kris said, "I need to talk to Mr. Blizzard for a minute before lunch ends. See you tomorrow, Elfis!" Kris held out his fist again and Elfis grinned and bumped it.

"See you, Kris." Elfis thought about what had just happened and how strange this last day had been.

Chapter 8

A Resolution

Elfis finished his lunch and looked over at the table where Ginger had been sitting. At some point while he had been talking to Kris she had gotten up and left. He thought to himself that she had probably gone to the workshop already to check in for work a bit early. He shrugged to himself disappointedly and started to clean up his area. He would see her at work and talk to her there.

Elfis kept thinking about everything she had said that morning. It wasn't true that she was the only one that finished their work, was it? And, if it was, that would make sense, right? After all, everyone knew it, even Kris had just mentioned it, she was the best toy maker in the school, and he wasn't very good no matter how much he tried. He always made mistakes, and was constantly putting the toys together incorrectly. And school was harder for him than it was for Ginger, but he cared about her. She was his best friend, and had been since they were little, the two of them did everything together.

As Elfis was thinking about all of this, he looked up and saw the school trophy case. All of the awards that students got were kept in here: best toymaker, school valedictorian, best athlete, most likely to succeed, etc. Elfis passed this thing every day but didn't ever stop to look at it. It always made him a little depressed, and it wasn't that tough to see why. Almost every trophy had his brother's name on it. Elfis loved his brother, and he was proud of him, but Frost was so cool, and so good at everything he did. Elfis couldn't measure up to his brother. It was easy to understand why his dad was disappointed with his second son.

Elfis stared at the trophy case lost in his own thoughts. He wasn't the best toymaker, or the best student, he knew that. But, if he was being honest with himself, he could try harder.

All he really was interested in was music. And, as long as he was being honest with himself, he could admit that one of the reasons he didn't try as hard as he should, one of the reasons he wasn't fully focused on his work, was because he knew that Ginger was there to fix things for him if he made a mistake. He did rely on her too much, as he knew how talented she was. Frost thought she was even a better toymaker than he was when he was in high school. It wasn't fair that she had to partner with him when he rarely helped her. The only thing he was really good at making were instruments, and she was probably better than him at making those too.

"Why are you looking at this dumb thing?" someone said behind Elfis, and he snapped out of his own thoughts. He turned around and was shocked to see Ginger behind him.

"Hey!" he said a bit too loudly. "What are you doing here?" he asked her.

"Where else would I be?" she responded.

"I assumed you went to the factory early when I didn't see you leave the cafeteria," Elfis said.

"No, I had to go talk to the principal about something real quick. Then I saw you standing here looking at the trophy case like it was the figure skating world trophy, and decided to see what was so captivating," Ginger replied.

"Frost is such a good toymaker," Elfis responded glumly. "And student. Why am I so bad at everything?" Elfis asked despondently.

"You're not bad at everything, E," Ginger said. "You just don't try hard enough at anything except snowball fights and guitar. You could be a really good toymaker if you focused on what you were making and stopped thinking about being a guitar player all the time."

"You're right," Elfis said. "Of course you're right, you're always right."

Ginger looked at him.

"You were even right this morning, Ginger. Kris helped me realize that today at lunch."

"Kris?" Ginger said, surprised. "How does Kris fit into all of this?"

"I'll tell you about that later, I couldn't believe it either," Elfis said. "But first, I need to apologize to you Ginger. I know I'm always thinking about the guitar and my music, and I know that it often leads to me making mistakes in school and at work, and the only thing that stops me from getting in trouble all the time is you. I'm sorry if I've been taking you for granted recently, you're my best friend and I need to start treating you the same way you've been treating me for our entire friendship. Sometimes I forget that even though you're the best toymaker we've got, you still might need my help occasionally," Elfis finished and let out a sigh.

Ginger stared at him for what felt like ten minutes, and

then took a step closer and gave him a big hug. "Thanks, E!" she said quietly into his shirt. "That means a lot."

"I was even thinking," Elfis continued, "that I would go to Mr. Jolly's office today and tell him that you need a new partner." Ginger looked at Elfis after he said this, clearly hurt.

"What are you talking about?" she demanded.

"It isn't fair to stick the best toymaker with the worst one, every day. You should be able to work with someone who can help you improve your skills, and won't slow you down every day," Elfis stammered.

"E, I want to work with you, I love working with you," "I just want you to try a little harder. If you do talk to Mr. Jolly about that today, you'll never be able to leave your house without being ambushed by snowballs everywhere you go, "And besides, you do help me improve my skills, fixing your mistakes is a great way to become a better toymaker," Ginger finished slyly, with a grin on her face.

Elfis looked at her and smiled. "I deserved that one," he said happily. Come on, let's get to work!"

The two elves chatted on their way to the workshop, both happy that they had resolved their issues. Elfis made a vow to himself that he was going to stop getting distracted, that he needed to buckle down and start focusing on his job and his grades. And, if he started to show some improvement his dad was far more likely to give him his guitar back sooner rather than later.

"Do you know what you're going to do for the talent show yet?" Elfis asked Ginger. "I completely forgot about it until Mr. Blizzard reminded us yesterday."

Ginger rolled her eyes, "Of course you did." She

laughed. "I've been thinking about it for a while. I would love to win, a sleigh ride to Iceland and a hundred candy canes. Not a bad prize, so I want to do something really creative, something no one else will have thought of."

"And?" Elfis asked. "Don't keep me in suspense, what are you going to make?"

"Well, I was thinking I'd make a miniature replica sleigh on stage, pulled by miniature robot reindeer," Ginger told him excitedly.

"What?" Elfis said. "How are you going to do that in the allotted ten-minute time frame? I know you're good, but that's way too little time to make a full replica sleigh with eight reindeer."

"You'll just have to wait and see," Ginger said mysteriously, and then laughed at the disappointed look on Elfis's face. "What about you?" Ginger asked him, knowing the answer before he gave it.

"Well, I was thinking about playing the guitar, and performing an Elvis show in full costume, but without my guitar I don't think that's doable any more," Elfis said, upset. "And it's not like I can practice either. Plus, as happy as my dad would be if I won it, I don't think he'll be thrilled with my talent being music, especially now. If I can't play the guitar, I may not even enter. I mean what else could I possibly do?" he asked rhetorically.

Ginger was saddened to hear this. "You've got to at least try, E. Even if you can't play guitar, you could make something too. Most of us are going to be making things after all, why not give it a shot?"

"And compete with you and your incredible working sleigh with reindeer?" Elfis chuckled without humor. "I wouldn't stand a chance. But you deserve to win, and I'll be in the audience cheering you on, you can count on that!" Elfis finished, trying to sound happy about not being able to participate in the talent show.

Ginger smiled at him, "Thanks E, what if we did something together though? You and I could enter as a duo, we could do the same thing I was already planning, but with your help I bet we could make all eight reindeer! We could possibly include Rudolph."

"No," Elfis said kindly but emphatically. "I would only mess it up for you, if we worked together. I'd much rather you win than both of us lose."

"Okay, but let's keep brainstorming over the next couple of days. I'm sure we can think of something for you to do before the submission deadline." The two continued chatting as they got to the workshop, this morning's argument entirely forgotten.

Chapter 9

Back to Work

When Elfis and Ginger got to the workshop, they saw that they had been assigned to Lego duty. (As a general rule, the elves disliked the Lego department. It didn't really require much imagination.) They figured Mr. Jolly had put them there as punishment, but they didn't care. Elfis must've stepped on twenty little rectangle pieces alone, but even that couldn't hurt his good mood. The two elves constructed thousands of little Lego pieces and chatted the entire time. Elfis didn't get distracted once and he didn't even mention the music being the same songs that they hear every day. All things considered, what had started as the worst day ever, with him in a fight with his dad and his best friend, turned out to not be so bad. The two finished work having completed their entire assignment and had put together enough extra pieces to construct the rocket ship. They finished work and headed home.

"So, Kris was actually nice to you for an entire lunch period?" Ginger asked.

"I couldn't believe it either, but we actually had a nice lunch," Elfis assured her. "He even mentioned the three of us hanging out sometime soon."

"Wow, the one day we don't sit together at lunch and

you end up becoming friends with the class bully!" Ginger laughed incredulously.

"I know," Elfis agreed. "Everything about today has been weird from start to finish."

As the two approached their houses, Elfis became a bit more somber. "My dad's still going to be mad at me. I haven't seen him since our argument last night," he told Ginger. So much had happened today that Elfis had almost forgotten about the night before.

"It'll be okay, E," Ginger reassured him. "He's had a day to cool off, and you had a great day at work today. He's probably as eager to move on from yesterday as you are."

Elfis, after the unfolding of events today, couldn't help but realize how Ginger really was always there for him. She was always so supportive whenever anything was wrong in his life. "Thanks Ginger," Elfis said, genuinely comforted at least partially by her words. She punched him on his shoulder and the two laughed. They fist-bumped and parted ways. "See you tomorrow before school!" Elfis shouted at her. She raised her hand in acknowledgement and Elfis smiled. He took a deep breath and slowly walked up his iceway to his house. He opened his door and Twinkle was waiting to pounce on him as soon as he did. He was caught off guard but managed to catch her and himself before the two of them fell over.

"Careful Twinkle, I almost dropped you," Elfis said smiling.

"Careful Twinkle, I almost dropped you," his sister mimicked in a low-pitched, poor imitation of Elfis. She looked up at him, waiting on him to talk so she could aggravate him some more.

"Really?" he asked her, and was unsurprised when she responded similarly. This was not a new game of his sister's, so Elfis decided to wait her out. He put his sister down and refused to say anything. Twinkle, who had an attention span similar to all three-year-olds, quickly got bored of waiting, blew a raspberry at her brother, and ran out of his room.

Elfis smiled to himself and shook his head, then he changed out of his work clothes and lay down on his bed. He couldn't prevent his gaze from turning to the now empty guitar stand, and he let out a depressed sigh when he saw it. Usually this is when he would get some practice time in. He only had nine more days to prepare for the talent show, and as he had never actually taken a guitar lesson, he needed all the practice he could get. "Well," he thought to himself, "I guess that doesn't matter any more." He threw on Elvis and just sat and listened to the King, while waiting for his dad and brother to get home from work. He could hear his mom rummaging around in the kitchen. She must be on the earlier shifts all week, Elfis assumed. With Twinkle only having a few hours of preschool a week, his parents rarely worked the same shifts any more. While he was anxiously waiting for his dad's arrival, he figured, since he had nothing else to do, he would get started on his homework. Last week Mr. Blizzard had assigned an essay describing their favorite toys and why they liked making them. It was due in two days, and Elfis remembered he hadn't started it yet.

He took out his notebook and started working. He soon heard the familiar sounds of his dad coming upstairs. Elfis let out a deep breath and figured he might as well get this done sooner rather than later.

"Hey Dad," Elfis said timidly. His father looked out from behind his closet door where he was hanging up his work clothes.

"Hey yourself, Elfis," his dad replied in a frosty tone. "How was work? Any rock concerts today?"

Elfis looked down, "No not today, I was in the Lego department, I feel like my shoes have permanent imprints in them after all the pieces I stepped on."

His father smiled. "I never much liked the Lego department either."

Encouraged, Elfis paused. "Dad, I'm sorry about what I said to you last night. It was out of line, and I was angry, and I didn't mean it."

Elfis's father looked at him for a full minute. The wait was unbearable. "Thank you Elfis, I appreciate you saying that." Elfis waited for his father to say more on the subject, but he didn't speak about it again.

After what felt like an eternity, Elfis got up his courage. "Dad," he said again.

"Yes," his father replied.

"I was wondering if maybe I could have my guitar back." He continued quickly before his father could interrupt him. "I'm really going to start buckling down in school and at work. In fact, Ginger and I had a long talk about how I'm going to help her out more and not get so distracted, and stop paying too much attention to my guitar and my music," he finished.

"Well," his father began. "I'm really glad to hear that. It's high time for you to start taking school and work seriously, and it makes me very happy to hear you recognize that as well. If you work for it, you can be as good a toymaker as your brother." His father stopped talking and Elfis waited expectantly. "As far as your guitar goes, no, Elfis, you can't have it back yet.

"But—" Elfis started to say, but his father interrupted him.

"I appreciate your apology, and I'm glad you are going to buckle down, but I need to see some proof. If you show me that you are serious, if you demonstrate to me that you are focusing on work, and your grades in school start to come up, then we can talk about you getting your guitar back, but until then, it's staying in the cupboard."

Elfis was crestfallen, he wanted to talk about it more, but he also figured that if he kept talking about the guitar his dad was even less likely to give it back. For now, he and his dad were not fighting, and he wanted to keep it that way. "Okay," he said.

"Go get ready for dinner, Elfis, your mom said it will be ready soon," his dad said, and he rubbed his son's head. "You're going to be okay." Elfis, discouraged, wasn't so sure.

Elfis walked back to his room. It looked like he really was going to have to get used to living his life without his guitar.

Chapter 10

Time to Buckle Down

Over the next several days, Elfis really did start to improve both his grades in school and his work at the factory. Mr. Blizzard even sent a note home to his parents telling him how focused he had been, and what a change he had already seen in Elfis's schoolwork. Elfis's parents were so pleased they promised his favorite frozen pasta dish for dinner. At work, he and Ginger were more productive than ever. Without his ever-present musical distraction, they were able to exceed their quota with time to spare. Kris had been spending more time with Elfis and Ginger as well, and the three of them were really getting along.

It wasn't until about five days later that Ginger started to think something might be wrong. Elfis, Ginger, and Kris were all walking home together, when Ginger asked if they wanted to have a snowball fight. Kris immediately jumped at the idea, but Elfis told her he was tired and just wanted to go home. In all the years they had been friends, Elfis had never once been too tired for a snowball fight. Ginger dropped the subject and the three continued walking. A few minutes later Kris turned toward his home, and as Ginger and Elfis were walking the remaining few blocks to their houses, Ginger asked if Elfis was okay.

"Yeah, I'm fine," Elfis said unconvincingly. "Why,

what's up?"

"Nothing," Ginger replied. "I was just curious, I've never seen you too tired for a snowball fight. No matter how many times I beat you, you keep fighting." Ginger hoped this playful joke would encourage Elfis to tell her what was wrong with him.

Elfis smiled at her. "First off, I don't lose that much." Ginger laughed at this. "But nothing's wrong, I just don't really want to have a snowball fight today."

"Okay," Ginger said. "Hey," she continued, changing the subject. "The deadline to submit the talent show application is only a couple of days away. Have you decided if you want to be a duo? I really think we can win. You've been doing so well at work recently, I think we could definitely get all eight reindeer made in the required time," Ginger said excitedly.

"Oh, I kind of forgot about that," Elfis said. "Sorry Ginger, I just don't think I want to be in the talent show. Besides, it will look better if you do it alone, it's more impressive, and I really think you've got a better chance at winning without me."

"Look, E, winning would be great, but it would also be a lot of fun to show everyone what we can do on stage. Just think about it over the next day or two, it'd be great to work together, and the deadline is coming up," Ginger encouraged him.

At that moment Elfis's front door opened and King raced out to meet the two elves. "Hey boy," Elfis said, and bent down to pat his head.

Ginger looked at him, and so did King. Elfis almost always picked King up and was usually a lot more enthusiastic when the fox met them as they were coming home from school. Ginger bent down and lifted up the arctic fox who appeared eternally grateful for the show of affection from her. "Good boy," Ginger said in a much more chipper tone. King licked her face and burrowed his nose into her coat. The two walked a little bit further, then Ginger reluctantly put the fox down and turned to go to her house. "See ya, E!" she said enthusiastically.

Elfis smiled at her. "Yeah, see you tomorrow!"

The two bumped fists and Ginger started walking towards her house. She was a little perturbed by how Elfis had been acting. He was usually in such a good mood, but today he seemed really down. She worried that maybe he was getting sick, or maybe, she thought, he was just really tired.

Elfis walked into his house with King still running circles around him. "Hey Dad," he yelled out. His father was on the earlier shifts now, so he was home to greet Elfis.

"Hey E," his father responded. "Your mom should be home in about an hour, I've got dinner almost finished so we'll eat as soon as she's back. You hungry?" Jack asked Elfis.

"Yeah, I am, sounds good Dad," Elfis responded and went upstairs to flop on his bed. As was part of his new routine, he looked at the empty guitar stand sadly and then flipped on his speaker.

"What's up, bro?" Elfis jumped as Frost poked his head into his room. "Did I wake you up?" he asked, grinning.

"No, I was just listening to music, I didn't hear you," Elfis responded to his brother. "How was work today? What'd you make?"

"I was making cars today," Frost said excitedly. "I always love making cars, they're so difficult, everything needs to be just right," he explained "What about you?"

"We were on sporting equipment today," Elfis answered his brother's question. "Not the most difficult department, but at least it's fun to test out what you've made," Elfis finished.

Frost cheerfully agreed. "Yeah, you're not kidding. Anyways, just letting you know, Mom should be home in like ten minutes, do you plan on eating in your work clothes tonight?"

Elfis looked down at what he was wearing, he had completely forgotten to change somehow. "Oh yeah." He half laughed at his brother. "Thanks Frost, I'll be down in a couple minutes." Frost winked at him and headed for the kitchen.

Elfis quickly changed his clothes and then he heard the front door open and his Mom's voice. "Dinner smells delicious!" she said happily. "Give me five minutes to unpack from work and then let's eat!"

Elfis changed out of his work clothes and went downstairs for dinner with his family. He walked down into the kitchen to find his family all seated around the table waiting for him.

"Took you long enough!" Twinkle said to him with a grin on her face.

"Sorry," Elfis replied. "I forgot to change out of my work clothes, I had a long day," Elfis said calmly and smiled at his sister.

"No problem, Elfis," his father said to him. "Have a seat." Elfis sat down and made himself a plate of the delicious meal his father had made for them tonight.

"How was work today?" Elfis's parents both asked him simultaneously and chuckled.

"What department were you in?" his mother finished.

"Ginger and I were in the sports department, we finished almost twice what we were supposed to do today. Mr. Jolly said he couldn't believe how much we got done!" Elfis finished.

"That's great!" his father said excitedly. "Mr. Jolly must be so pleased with how you two are doing!"

"Yeah," Elfis responded nonchalantly to his father, "he was pretty happy with us."

Elfis's father couldn't help but notice Elfis's lack of enthusiasm. "Well, I'm glad to hear you're doing so well recently, it really shows you've matured and are taking your work seriously, finally."

Elfis's mother touched her husband's arm and looked at him out of the corner of her eye. "Okay Jack, Elfis is doing a great job," she said deliberately. Jack saw something in her face that made him change the subject.

"How was school, sweetie?" Elfis's mother asked him.

"It was good, I got an A on my North Pole history paper and I've already turned in my essay due on Friday."

"Great job, E," Frost interjected, and gave him a high five.

"Thanks," Elfis responded. "We also talked about the talent show a lot, everyone seems to be entering, it's going to be really tough to win the prize!" Elfis finished, sounding a bit more enthusiastic.

"Are you still planning on sitting the talent show out?" Jack asked him.

"I am, I don't know what I would do, and I don't really have enough time to figure something out now," Elfis responded.

"I still don't get why you don't team up with Ginger?" Elfis's mom asked. "I think that would give you a great chance at taking first prize. The two of you would be hard to beat, who's more talented than you two?"

"I already told you, Mom," Elfis said. "It will look better if it's just one person, and besides, Ginger doesn't need my help."

Elfis's mom sighed, she didn't want to see her son sitting out of the talent show, as he had been so excited for it only a week or two ago. Plus, Frost had won the talent show only a few years earlier, and she thought it would be good for her younger son to enter as well. "Elfis," she hesitated, "a couple of weeks ago you told me you had the best idea for the talent show." Elfis looked up at his mother while she was talking. "Why don't you want to do that any more?"

Elfis took a big gulp of water, and when he put the cup down, his mother noticed that he glanced at his father nervously before answering. "I don't know, Mom, maybe my idea wasn't such a good one. I thought I could've won, but it doesn't matter any more," Elfis finished sadly.

"What was your idea, E?" Elfis's father asked him, showing concern, as his son was never this close-mouthed and quiet, so Jack started to get a little worried.

"Nothing," Elfis responded. Jack started to ask Elfis about his idea further when Twinkle interrupted.

"He was going to put on a guitar show for everyone, duh," she said smugly. "He was going to dress up like the king and everything." Twinkle finished giggling as she said it.

Elfis glared at her. "Twinkle, shut up! I'm not doing that, Dad," Elfis tried to explain himself. "I told you, I'm not going to enter the competition."

Twinkle had stopped smiling, in fact she started to look weepy after her brother told her to shut up. Elfis's mom rubbed her hair to calm her down. "Elfis, don't tell your sister to shut up."

Jack looked down at his son. "You were going to perform a rock concert huh?" he asked.

"It was just an idea I had. It doesn't matter," Elfis finished quietly.

"No, I guess it doesn't," Jack replied. The conversation around the dinner table faltered as everyone continued to eat their food.

After a minute or two, Elfis, having eaten enough, asked to be excused. "Can I go up to my room? I've got some homework to finish up before tomorrow."

"Go ahead," his mother responded worriedly to him. Elfis cleared his plate, went upstairs, and collapsed on his bed. He looked sadly at his guitar case and thought about the talent show that was only three days away now. The deadline to enter was tomorrow morning, and while he hadn't expected his dad to give him his guitar back, he kept hoping that he would have it back in time for the talent show. However, he had seen his father's face when his sister brought up playing guitar for the talent show. He had not been amused, and things were finally going well between the two of them. He hadn't gotten in trouble recently and had been doing great both in school and at work. He had hoped that with his recent improvements his father would give him back his instrument, but after what happened at dinner, he didn't think that was happening any time soon. Elfis looked over at his picture of the King live at Memphis and couldn't help but feel depressed. This last week without his guitar had been one of the more difficult weeks he could remember having.

"Jack?" Holly started, later that night, as the two were clearing up the kitchen and getting ready for bed.

"What's up?" Jack answered his wife.

"I'm worried about Elfis." Jack looked at her and she continued, "He hasn't seemed himself lately, has he? He's been so quiet and unenthusiastic recently, and tonight at dinner he seemed so upset."

Jack sighed before answering his wife. "I know what you mean," he admitted. "Ever since I took his guitar away, he's been in a funk. But look at how he's been doing since then!" Jack was quick to point out. "In just the week since he's been without his guitar his grades are up and his work has improved. Without his guitar he's not as distracted and is doing so much better."

"I know, Jack," Holly replied, "but he just seems so sad and down now. Is it worth it? I don't want my son to be miserable all the time."

Jack took a deep breath. "I don't want him to be miserable either, but he just misses his guitar. In another week or so I am sure he will have forgotten all about his instrument and he'll be back to his normal, happy self. I'm sure of it," Jack finished confidently.

"I hope you're right, Jack, I can't stand to see Elfis so

down all the time."

"If his work continues to improve and he keeps doing well in school, I'll give him his guitar back, but for now, he's doing just fine without it," Jack continued. "Plus, you heard what Twinkle said, he was planning on playing guitar for the talent show. Can you believe that? He'd be the only elf not making toys up on the stage. That's proof that he was taking his music too seriously and ignoring his actual responsibilities. I know he's sad right now, but this will be good for him in the long run. He can't keep thinking about his music, but when he learns to balance his responsibilities with his hobbies, he can have his guitar back," Jack finished emphatically.

"Okay," Holly agreed. "I suppose it's for the best, but Jack, if he stays this miserable it won't matter how well he's doing in school or at work, he'll be too upset to enjoy anything." Jack looked solemnly at his wife and nodded at her. Whatever face they tried to put on, it was clear they both were worried about their son.

Chapter 11

A Surprise Encounter

Elfis woke up the next morning feeling even worse than when he had gone to bed. He had dreamed that he was in The North Pole Pavilion in front of thousands of elves, as well as Santa and Mrs. Claus. He walked out to tumultuous applause and as he was getting ready to give them the best rock show anyone had ever seen, he looked down at his hands to find that there was no guitar there. Elfis looked over at the stage manager who looked at him questioningly. Elfis looked out at the crowd who was starting to get anxious now. The applause that had first greeted him had died down and there was some confused mumbling from the crowd. Elfis nervously tried to find a guitar anywhere on stage, when he was hit in the back by a snowball launched from a daring concertgoer. As is the way of these things, that first snowball led to a barrage of well-aimed snowballs from frustrated and angry elves. Elfis jerked out of this nightmare in a cold sweat and waited a minute while the vivid reality of this dream dissipated. As it did, he slowly got out of bed and got ready for another day without music.

Ginger met Elfis outside her house and the two walked to school. It was a beautiful morning, brisk and cold. The two walked to school chatting about the talent show, and what they were going to do in school that day, but it did not escape Ginger's notice that her best friend was still not his usual self. Throughout the entire school day Ginger decided to keep an eye on Elfis. If he was not better tomorrow, she made a promise to herself that she would talk to the school principal and try to figure out what was going on with her best friend.

The school day passed largely without incident and after the three elves ate lunch (at this point Kris was always found at their lunch table talking and laughing as if there had never been an issue between the three teenagers), Elfis announced he was going to take the day off work.

"What do you mean?" Ginger asked Elfis.

"Are you sick?" Kris asked, with a look of concern on his face.

"I can't go to work today," Elfis said flatly. "I need a day off. Can you guys tell Mr. Jolly I won't be in today?"

"Sure," the two elves said at the same time and exchanged an uncomfortable smile. It wasn't the not going to work they were concerned with. Elves were encouraged to take days off work when they needed one, and it was said Santa made this rule centuries ago in order to keep elves from getting burned out, and to keep the quality of the workshop and toys of the highest caliber. It was a testament to how much elves love their work that this policy was rarely used and had not even once been taken advantage of. The two friends knew that if Elfis was using this day off, that he really needed it. Mr. Jolly would understand as well.

Ginger and Kris headed to the factory after giving Elfis a high five and he watched them as they disappeared in a sea of snow. He wasn't sure where he wanted to go, but he knew he couldn't work today, and he didn't want to go home. Elfis couldn't decide what to do with his afternoon off. He wasn't sick, but he certainly wasn't well. Elfis's feet started to walk in a random direction and Elfis had no choice but to follow them. As his feet walked seemingly of their own volition, Elfis was lost in his own thoughts, not knowing or particularly caring where he ended up. As he walked, he started thinking about his dream again, as well as how depressed he had been without his guitar this last week. He thought to himself, never knowing that his parents had basically mirrored this line of thought in their conversation the night before, that ever since his guitar was taken away, his grades and work had been a lot better, but he had been miserable. He had tried to put on a brave face, tried to act like it didn't matter, but every day he saw that empty guitar stand was like a raw wound opening back up. He couldn't help but wonder why it mattered if he was a good toymaker, or the best student, if he couldn't enjoy those accomplishments.

As Elfis was walking and thinking, he heard a rumble of thunder coming from the distance. The roar was loud enough to bring him out of his own mind, but not so loud that it was about to start raining. Elfis looked up at the sky confused. There wasn't a cloud anywhere on the horizon, so where had that thunder come from? As Elfis listened for another rumble he heard it again, but this time it didn't stop, it was continuous, and as Elfis really paid attention he realized it wasn't thunder at all. His feet had taken him to the reindeer park without him knowing, and it wasn't thunder he was hearing, but reindeer running in tandem. He hadn't been to the park in years, not since his family took a day trip here when Twinkle was a year old, but he loved this park. The reindeer were magical beasts, and if you were lucky, you could see a reindeer jump over the trees, and on very rare occasions, you could even see one of them fly around a bit. That was a treat he had never witnessed, but few had. Reindeer usually flew only when they were attached to the sleigh.

The reindeer had cheered Elfis up and he continued walking with a bit more spring in his step. A bit ahead of him, he noticed a figure in a red coat leaning against a tree. Intrigued, Elfis walked closer until he was able to make out the long silver hair of Mrs. Claus watching a group of three reindeer drink from an ice-cold lake.

Elfis stopped as soon as he recognized who was at the tree. He didn't want to interrupt Mrs. Claus and he was getting ready to turn around and walk away when he stepped on a branch, and it snapped. He stopped and Mrs. Claus, startled, turned around and saw him trying to avoid notice. Mrs. Claus was a legend and despite her reputation for kindliness, Elfis felt intimidated by her presence. Elfis had only seen her once at her traditional welcome to the incoming class of high school freshmen, but other than listening to her speak, he had never actually met or spoken to the woman who everyone said ran the North Pole.

"Well, how lovely of you to join me," Mrs. Claus said, and Elfis turned around and looked directly at Mrs. Claus.

"Me?"

"Well, I don't see anyone else around, do you?" Mrs. Claus spoke very kindly, with a gentle tone, but appeared to be a no-nonsense individual. Elfis was easily able to imagine how this woman kept the North Pole running so smoothly. "Come on over and watch these reindeer," she continued, and her tone left no room for argument. Elfis nervously walked over and stood beside the commanding woman.

Elfis didn't know what to say, or even if he should say anything at all. Here was one of the two most famous people in the North Pole, probably in the world, and Elfis for the first time in his life was standing next to her, completely tongue-tied, watching reindeer.

Mrs. Claus smiled down at him, knowing she was more than a little intimidating, and she couldn't help but be amused by the situation. "You look like you should be at work or school right about now, what are you doing here?"

"Yes ma'am," said Elfis. "I was just on my way to the workshop, I must have taken a wrong turn, I'm heading there now," Elfis lied. He thought to himself that if ever there was a time to meet Mrs. Claus up close and personal, this was the worst possible moment. He wanted to extricate himself from this situation as soon as possible.

"I'm sure you are," Mrs. Claus said unconvinced, and studied the young elf for what seemed like hours. "But as you're probably already quite late for wherever you are supposed to be, why don't you park it, and watch these beautiful creatures with me?" she finished and smiled as if she knew exactly what he had been thinking.

"So, how are you, Elfis?" Mrs. Claus said after a minute or so of silence.

Elfis looked up at her too astonished to reply.

"Surprised, are you?" Mrs. Claus answered the unasked question, with a smile. "I don't see you all nearly enough, but that doesn't mean I don't know each and every one of you!" She finished kindly.

"Oh," Elfis stammered out. "I'm okay, ma'am."

Mrs. Claus let out a rich, full laugh at this, the sound of which immediately put Elfis more at ease. "Please, Mrs. Claus," she said. "No one ever calls me ma'am."

"Sorry ma'am, I mean, Mrs. Claus."

She laughed again. "So, what brings you to the park today? And don't tell me you took a wrong turn on your way to work!" she finished.

"I was just walking, not really paying attention, just thinking, and this is where I ended up," Elfis said with a shrug. He couldn't believe he was having a casual conversation with THE Mrs. Claus.

"Why aren't you at work?" Mrs. Claus asked. Elfis listened for any condemnation in her voice but couldn't hear any.

"I just couldn't go today, I'm not sure why."

Mrs. Claus looked at Elfis, and the compassion in her eyes eased his trepidation about opening up to her. "Why not?"

"It's kind of a long story," Elfis said to Mrs. Claus.

"Well, as you're clearly not going to work, and I've got some free time on my hands, why don't you tell me this long story," she said.

Elfis looked up at Mrs. Claus and amazingly, he started to tell her everything that had happened over the last week or so. Mrs. Claus listened impassively to this young elf's tale while reindeer ran around the two of them serenely.

"And now, I am doing better in school, and my work has gotten loads better. I hardly ever make mistakes that Ginger has to fix, but I can't stop thinking about my guitar.

I feel sad all the time, and I just don't seem to have any energy at all. And I don't want to tell my dad any of this because I don't want him to get upset with me again. I know how much he hates my guitar." Elfis finished his story, and Mrs. Claus continued to look down at him with another of those long, weighing stares that seemed to go on forever. It was all Elfis could do not to fidget under her gaze.

Finally, Mrs. Claus broke the silence. "So, Jack hates the guitar now?" she said under her breath, and then more loudly to Elfis, "Well, you certainly have a lot going on, don't you?" Elfis nodded at her, but he didn't want to talk, as telling his story had left him on the verge of tears and he couldn't bear to cry in front of Mrs. Claus.

"How long have you been playing the guitar?"

Elfis composed himself and answered Mrs. Claus. "My entire life, it's my favorite thing to do," he admitted.

"Are you any good?" Mrs. Claus asked, and this struck Elfis as an odd question.

"I think I am," he answered. "But I rarely get to play in front of other people, so I guess I don't know for sure. But Ginger says I'm good!" he finished as if in defense of his guitar skills.

"You know, Santa loves making toys," Mrs. Claus said. Elfis looked up at her. Seconds ago they had been talking about Elfis and his guitar, and as if she had been listening to another conversation, Mrs. Claus was talking about her husband and toys. Was this kind, powerful woman losing it? Did she even hear what he had just said? Mrs. Claus looked down at him, almost as if she knew what he had been thinking. "Don't interrupt," her eyes seemed to say as they sparkled from the reflection of the snow.

"For centuries he worked and built toys in the workshop, and he loved every minute of it," she continued. "And for a while, he was the best toymaker too. Now even the newest elf can make toys better and more efficiently, but it wasn't always that way. Toys have become more complicated, and he is too busy to spend much time in the workshop, but when Santa only had to fly one day a year, he spent a lot of his time in the workshop." Elfis was equal parts confused about why Mrs. Claus was telling him this, and curious as to where the story was going.

Mrs. Claus continued, "When the workload got to be too much for Mr. Claus, when the orders started to back up, and more and more of his nights were spent delivering things, he wasn't able to continue making toys. He was too busy, and in any event, he wasn't really needed in the workshop. So, we decided that he would hand off all of his workshop duties to Mr. Jolly."

"I didn't know any of that!" Elfis exclaimed. At this point he was so engaged in the story that he forgot to be nervous about being next to Mrs. Claus.

"It's true," Mrs. Claus continued, "and it worked out well." She paused and looked down at Elfis. "At least at first." Elfis looked up at her confused. "Santa was so busy that I didn't notice anything right away. But eventually I started to realize that he wasn't his jolly, outgoing self. He stopped paying as much attention to the reindeer, he was more tired than usual, and although he tried to put on a brave face, I could tell something was wrong with him.

"Well," Mrs. Claus continued, "eventually I realized what the problem was. Santa was sad about not making toys any more. As important as he is to all of us here at the North

Pole and everyone living down south, he just wasn't entirely happy if he wasn't making toys." Mrs. Claus finished her story and Elfis looked up at her confused.

"That's it?" Elfis said before he could stop himself, and quickly looked away, embarrassed by his outburst.

Mrs. Claus let out a rich laugh and patted Elfis's head. "Not quite. It took me a while to figure out what to do, but I couldn't stand to see Santa so upset, and unfortunately, there wasn't time for him to be in the workshop, it didn't make any sense. But I finally figured out the solution." Elfis was listening eagerly again. "I made Santa his very own workshop attached to our house. Just a little one, it's just one room, but it has all his equipment and tools he needs for making toys. And, every Saturday, Santa spends the entire day making toys. Some of them he makes for humans, some for elves, sometimes he makes things for the reindeer, and sometimes he makes toys just for us. But we make sure that Saturdays are just for him to do what he loves to do. Ever since we created his own personal toy room, we haven't had any issues. Santa doesn't feel bad about not making toys, he's not taking up space and making mistakes in the workshop, and all of his work gets done on time and up to his usual standards!" Mrs. Claus finished.

"Oh," Elfis said. "Cool," he finished, rather anticlimactically. He couldn't understand why Mrs. Claus had just told him this long story. He had been hoping for help with his problem but was instead treated to an admittedly very interesting story, but also one that didn't help him much.

Some of Elfis's disappointment must have shown on his face, because Mrs. Claus continued her story. "So, you see

Elfis, Santa was born to make toys, it's what he loves to do, but it was getting in the way of the North Pole's efficiency, and his desire to keep making toys was leading to problems. But I also didn't want to prevent Santa from making toys, as I had already seen what happened when he couldn't create, and I didn't want to go back to that again. So, we found a balance. Saturdays are for Santa and his toys, and the rest of the week, he is taking care of everything else we need him for," she finished, smiling down at Elfis.

Elfis was embarrassed to admit to himself that he still didn't know what Mrs. Claus was talking about. Fortunately, she elaborated even further. "If playing the guitar is what you were born to do, and without it, you won't be happy, then you need to find a balance. I'm sure that's all your father wants from you. Playing the guitar is fine, in fact, I love the guitar, but it can't be the only thing you think about all the time. When you are in your house after work is a great time to play. As are weekends. When you're in school though, you should be thinking about school, not the guitar. When you are in the middle of a shift during work…" She paused with a twinkle in her eye. "Maybe that's not the best time to stage a rock concert," she finished, smiling.

Elfis looked up at Mrs. Claus astonished. "You know about that?" Elfis asked, ashamed.

Mrs. Claus smiled down at him and nodded. "So, what do you say? Can you find that balance? Hobbies and passions are important, but they aren't all that's important, and, knowing your father like I do…" Elfis was surprised at this statement, although he realized from this story that maybe there's nothing that goes on in the North Pole that

Mrs. Claus didn't know about. "I'm sure the two of you can reach an agreement and you can get your guitar back."

Elfis was about to thank Mrs. Claus for telling him this story and talking with him, when he heard a sound coming out of the trees unlike anything he had already heard that day. It wasn't the galloping of hooves or the neigh of a reindeer, but it was a low, loud shout. Elfis looked around nervously, but Mrs. Claus seemed completely unperturbed. "Um, Mrs. Claus, do you know what that noise is?"

"That man," Mrs. Claus said, so quietly that Elfis wasn't sure he even heard anything. Mrs. Claus looked down at Elfis. "Oh," she said in a much more audible tone. "Don't worry dear, it's just Santa."

Elfis started to ask Mrs. Claus why Santa was yelling in the reindeer park, when at that very moment a huge reindeer came trotting out of the trees with Santa half running, half being dragged along by the reindeer. He had gotten his arm caught in the reins and he was only wearing one shoe, and it didn't take long for Elfis to see why. Somehow in the reindeer's mouth was a big red shoe that clearly belonged on Santa's other foot.

"Stop it you silly beast!" Santa was shouting good naturedly. "Give me back my shoe," he commanded the reindeer, who took no notice of one of the most magical people on the planet clinging onto his back. "Help me dear!" Santa shouted when he saw his wife.

After everything that had happened over the last week or so, Elfis couldn't help himself. Seeing Santa being dragged around the reindeer park with only one shoe on, he burst into a fit of hysterical laughter. Mrs. Claus smiled down at the elf and went to help her husband. By the time she had calmed down the reindeer, untied Santa from the reins he had somehow trapped himself in, and retrieved his shoe from the animal, Elfis had fallen down in the snow and was clutching his side from laughter.

The two most important and powerful people in the North Pole walked over to the still laughing elf and helped him up out of the snow. As Elfis stood up and brushed the snow off himself, he apologized to Santa for laughing, while still trying not to laugh at what he had just seen.

"Nonsense my boy," Santa said to him in a booming, jovial voice. "Laughter is what keeps the North Pole up and running smoothly," he said.

"Elfis and I were just having a little talk, Santa," Mrs. Claus filled her husband in. "He's been having kind of a rough week, he had his guitar taken away."

"Well, I'm sorry to hear that, Elfis. I once played the guitar, did you know that?"

"What do you mean you played the guitar?" Mrs. Claus interrupted before Elfis could answer. "You tried to play one time, broke two strings, and somehow hit yourself in the knee with the guitar head. You limped for a week." Elfis couldn't help but laugh at this story.

Santa smiled at the memory. "That is how that ended, isn't it?" He laughed.

Mrs. Claus looked exasperated with her husband. "Well, Elfis, I really enjoyed our visit today. But I think it's time for you to head home and speak to your father, don't you?"

"Yes, thanks Mrs. Claus, I really liked talking to you too." he said sincerely. "Bye Santa, great to see you too!"

"You as well my boy," he boomed out.

"And remember, Elfis," Mrs. Claus said as Elfis was getting ready to leave, "when you find that balance we talked about, I think everything will get better for you!" Elfis smiled and nodded, thanked Mrs. Claus one more time, and started to walk home.

"Honey," Elfis heard Santa ask as he was walking, "have you seen my hat?"

"Oh, for goodness's sake," Mrs. Claus said. "If you've let a reindeer eat another hat of yours…" Elfis laughed to himself as the two of them continued to bicker good naturedly. Today had been one of the strangest days he'd ever had, and that was saying something. Elfis resolved to speak to his dad tonight when he got home, and, he thought, if everything went well, he could be getting his guitar back tonight. As he walked home, for the first time in more than a week, Elfis felt confident and happy.

Chapter 12

Finding a Balance

Elfis arrived at his house earlier than usual, and he was unsurprised to find himself home alone. Both his parents and his brother were most likely at the workshop, and his sister would still be at daycare. Elfis decided to use this quiet time to work out a plan for approaching his dad.

A little while later Elfis heard the front door open, and his sister ran inside and let out a shriek at King who jumped up and licked her face. "Get down King," Twinkle said to the fox. Elfis heard his dad follow his sister into the house and went down to greet the two of them.

"Hey Dad," Elfis said.

"Elfis, what are you doing home so early?" his father asked him.

"I took the day off work, I wasn't feeling very well after school," Elfis explained.

"Oh no," his father said. "Is everything okay?"

"Not yet," Elfis said, "But I think it will be soon. Can we talk, Dad?"

"Okay," Elfis's father said, clearly a little confused about how his son was acting. "Give me five minutes and then I'll meet you in the living room."

A few minutes later Elfis found himself face to face with his father and couldn't help but feel nervous about what he was going to ask. Rather than come right out and say it, he decided to work up to asking his father for his guitar back. "Guess who I ran into today?"

"Who?" his father asked.

"Santa and Mrs. Claus," Elfis responded excitedly. "I was going for a walk and saw Mrs. Claus leaning against a tree, we watched the reindeer and talked for a while and then Santa showed up!" Elfis recounted the entire story to his father and was happy to hear his father burst into laughter when he told the part about Santa coming out of the trees. "Did you know Santa used to build toys, Dad?"

"As a matter of fact. I did," his father said, smiling down at his son.

The two elves looked at each other for a moment. "Mrs. Claus kept talking about finding a balance, and how it took Santa a while after he stopped making toys to be happy again."

"That Mrs. Claus is one smart woman, she's the real brains behind the operation," Jack said and winked at Elfis, who chuckled. Elfis was just getting ready to ask the question that had been weighing on him for the last week, but before he did, his dad spoke up. "You know, I used to play the guitar."

Elfis was speechless. Jack, seeing the look of incredulity in his son's face, couldn't help but laugh. "It's true, when I was a little older than you, I was actually in a band with a few friends."

"Were you guys any good?" It was all Elfis could say, he was still trying to process this new piece of information. His father, the man who took his guitar away and seemed to hate music, had actually been in a band.

"We sure weren't," Jack responded smiling. "We were pretty mediocre, and after we had been playing together for a couple of years, the band broke up."

"Why?"

"Well, we had to focus on work, I met your mother, and the guys with me in the band decided it was the right thing to do. For them, music was just a fun hobby. We weren't very good, like I said, and we had real futures to think about. So, the band broke up, and for the other guys it was just a fun memory. But, for me, music was always something more. It wasn't just a hobby for me, it was all I cared about. I never told the elves in the band, but when we broke up, I was devastated."

Elfis couldn't believe any of what he was hearing. He would be less surprised if he found out Santa hated milk and cookies. "You could have kept playing alone," he suggested to his father.

"I did for a little bit, but eventually I had to realize that I was never going to be a professional musician. I wasn't good enough, and for me, playing the guitar just made me feel really sad. It made me feel like I had given up on my dreams. It took years before I was finally able to put music in my past and look forward at my life and what awaited me. And since then, your mother and I have gotten married, I've become a great toymaker, and we have the three best elves in the world as children," Elfis's dad finished on a positive note.

"Do you ever miss playing the guitar?" Elfis asked his father. He wasn't sure where this conversation was going, but it felt good to be open and honest with his dad.

"Sometimes I do, I love the guitar. You know, it was my

idea to name you after Elvis, your mom wanted to name you Fluffy." Elfis's dad looked down at his son and was happy to be able to finally tell him all of this. "The point is, E, the day I finally realized that I had no future as a musician, that I was maybe not as good as I thought or hoped I was, that was one of the most difficult days of my life. I had set my sights on being a rock star, and when I had to give up that dream it crushed me." Elfis started to see what his father was getting at. "When I saw that you had that same passion for music that I once had, I didn't want you to have to go through the same thing that I did all of those years ago."

The two elves were quiet for a couple minutes, the only sound was Twinkle playing with King in the next room over. "That's why you took my guitar away?" Elfis asked.

"Well, I took your guitar away for the reasons we talked about, but I may have overreacted. And, I should never have taken your guitar away without telling you this story. I don't want to stifle your creative passion, and I certainly don't want you to be miserable all the time. But I also wanted to protect you from the terrible ordeal I went through," his dad finished.

Elfis was seeing his dad in an entirely new way, and, as a result, he felt closer to him than he ever had before. "But Dad, if you never let me try to be a guitar player, then how will I know if I am good enough, or if I could ever be a rockstar. Maybe in a few years I will have to hang up my guitar for good, but isn't it important that I figure all of that out for myself? I may have the same journey as you did, but I could also have a completely different one. And I'll never get to find out if I am good enough if you keep my guitar," Elfis continued, trying to modify his tone so as not to sound like he was accusing his father of anything. "I would rather try and fail, than not try at all. It won't make me any sadder or more depressed in a few years than I am or have been this past week or so. I have to be able to try, Dad!" Elfis finished, almost pleading with his father.

Jack looked down at his son for what felt like an eternity. Finally, he stood up abruptly, catching Elfis off guard, and walked out of the room. Elfis was confused, an emotional state that was all too common in his life recently, and as he was getting up to follow his father out of the room, Jack walked back into the room holding Elfis's guitar.

"Do I get it back?" Elfis all but shouted, unable to control himself.

"With one condition," Jack said to his son. "Everything we talked about at dinner the other night still holds. If your schoolwork starts to drop again, or if there is another midday concert at the workshop, I'm taking it away and you'll be my age before you play the guitar again. But I shouldn't have taken this away from you without a proper explanation, and I am sorry that I did, but your behavior has to be better. Just like Mrs. Claus said, you need to be able to find a balance. You have shown me that you are capable of excelling both at work and at school, so if you can maintain that balance, and keep up the good work, I don't see why you can't have your guitar back."

Elfis couldn't believe this. Only a few hours ago he was sure he was never going to play the guitar again and now he was getting back his most prized possession. "Thanks Dad!" he said, enveloping his father in a big hug. "Don't worry, I'm done getting distracted!" he assured his father. Jack hugged his son back and then Elfis ran up to his room to make sure the guitar was in proper working order.

Elfis was still shocked. It had only been a week without his guitar, but that week had felt like an eternity. He immediately played a few chords and fixed the couple of strings that were mildly out of tune, and he couldn't stop smiling. Elfis spent the rest of his afternoon getting reacquainted with his guitar. He briefly lamented the fact that he wouldn't be able to enter the talent show, as signups had already closed, but he thought to himself at least he had his guitar back. And he thought that he had finally reached an understanding with his dad. In all of the excitement of the afternoon, between meeting Santa and Mrs. Claus, and getting his instrument back, he hadn't fully appreciated what his father had told him. He wanted to be a rockstar too? No wonder Elfis loved music so much, he had inherited that from his dad!

Later in the evening, Elfis reluctantly put his guitar back on his stand to complete his homework. He didn't want to jeopardize this new relationship with his dad already, and he was determined to find the proper balance between his guitar and his work. Everything that had happened in the last six hours had really made him realize that he had been focusing too much on being a musician. He had to focus on his school and his job too, and it was a lesson Elfis was not going to forget anytime soon. After finishing his schoolwork Elfis got into bed really happy for the first time in over a week!

Chapter 13

Preparation

Elfis woke up the next morning and took a quick look at his guitar stand to make sure the events from the previous evening hadn't all been a dream. He was relieved to see his guitar back where it belonged. Elfis got up and went downstairs to have breakfast with his family. As he was getting ready, Elfis felt another twinge of sadness at the fact that tonight was the talent show, and he wouldn't be participating. However, Elfis wasn't going to let that feeling prevent him from cheering on Ginger. It would be great if she won, Elfis thought to himself, and she should be a shoo-in given how skilled she was and what she was going to be doing!

After eating a huge breakfast – Saturday breakfast was a tradition in Elfis's household, as that was the only day the family ate all together with no one being rushed – Elfis decided to go knock on Ginger's door.

Ginger's mother answered. "Good morning, Elfis," she greeted him, with a hug. "How are you, sweetie?" Elfis braced himself, her hugs were way too tight, and always left Elfis feeling like his spine had been realigned.

"Good morning, Mrs. Tinsel," Elfis replied, mentally checking to make sure all of his bones were still intact. "Is Ginger here?" he asked.

"She is, she's just doing some last-minute practice for the talent show tonight," she explained. "You guys must be so excited!"

"Well," Elfis said, "I'm not actually participating tonight, I couldn't think of what to do." Elfis covered up the actual reason he wasn't going to be in the talent show, and, seeing Ginger's mother's reaction, he was once again hit with a wave of sadness that he wouldn't be participating.

"Oh, that's a shame, Elfis, the talent show is such a fun and rewarding experience," Mrs. Tinsel said, unintentionally making Elfis feel worse.

"Yeah, well there's always next year," Elfis said, trying to sound optimistic.

"Of course there is dear," Mrs. Tinsel reassured him. "Ginger is downstairs, you know the way."

Elfis showed himself to the basement where he found Ginger hard at work. She glanced up when she heard his footsteps and smiled at him. "What's up, E?"

Ginger looked as if she had already been up for hours practicing. "Ginger, did you get any sleep at all?"

She rolled her eyes at Elfis, "Of course I did, I've just been practicing putting together small machines, as I'm still a little worried about the timing tonight. I've decided that in my model I'm going to try and make all eight reindeer rather than four, so I need to be extra fast, and doubly careful."

"Ginger, you're going to win this thing," Elfis reassured her. "Even if you only had four reindeer. You need to relax a little bit, you don't want to tire yourself out before the show." She looked at him skeptically over the model she was working on. "You need to find a proper balance," Elfis said, trying to be wise.

Ginger stared at him for a minute and smiled. "What on earth are you talking about?" she asked him.

"Oh nothing, just something Mrs. Claus said to me yesterday."

That stopped Ginger cold. "What?" she almost shouted. "When did all of this happen?"

Elfis laughed. "Yeah, yesterday was a crazy day. Come on, take a break from your work, let's go for a walk and get some air and I'll tell you all about it."

Ginger was reluctant to take a break, as she would much rather have kept practicing, but she had to hear this story. "Okay," she finally said, "Let's walk down to the school and see if the times for tonight have been posted yet." This was elf tradition, that on the day of the talent show there was a board posted on the front door of the school announcing when each elf would perform.

Elfis agreed, but he would rather have not gone to the school, where there were sure to be dozens of his classmates all with the same idea as Ginger. Elfis didn't want to be constantly reminded that he wasn't going to be participating in the show tonight, but he needed to support Ginger, and he was going to, plus, he really wanted to tell her this story.

Elfis recounted his tale as the two walked to school, and Ginger was appropriately amazed by what Elfis considered the weirdest, and most eventful afternoon of his life. "And you got your guitar back!" she said as he finished up.

As the school came into view, Elfis saw exactly what he had been hoping to avoid. He could see several of his classmates and elves from other grades and classes all trying to see when they were going to perform this evening.

As the two approached the school Elfis paused. "I'll wait here," he said. "You go check your time, I'll hang back, it's a little crowded." Ginger went on ahead and Elfis waited morosely.

A couple of minutes later Ginger returned. "So, when are you on?" Elfis asked her.

"I'm not sure, I think there may be a misprint on the sheet," Ginger said.

"What do you mean?"

"Well, I can't find my name, can you come help me look for it?" Ginger was acting strange, and Elfis knew why. If there had been some mistake and Ginger wasn't performing, Elfis didn't know what he could do, but he knew he would have to do something. Ginger had worked too hard and was too talented to not be able to perform tonight.

Elfis hesitantly walked up to the notice board to look, and he saw her name almost immediately. She was scheduled for seven thirty that night. Elfis had no clue how she had missed her name, but he figured maybe she was just nervous and overlooked it. He looked at the paper one more time to double check he had seen it correctly and paused. Underneath Ginger's name, a few slots down, for the final performance of the night, he saw his own name. He stared at it and rubbed his eyes to make sure he wasn't seeing things.

"I wanted you to be able to participate tonight," Ginger said from behind him. He hadn't realized she had followed him. "I didn't think it was fair for you to have to sit in the audience all night and not be able to showcase your talent."

Elfis was silent, and Ginger was worried that he was

angry with her. "We can talk to Mr. Blizzard and see if he can erase your name," Ginger said. "I'm sure that's an option, E. I'm sorry, Elfis, I should have told you what I was doing, but I just thought you would regret it if you didn't sign up."

Elfis took two steps towards Ginger and wrapped her in a hug that would have been too tight even for her mother. Ginger hugged him back but couldn't help feeling a little confused. "All morning I've been trying to avoid thinking about the talent show," Elfis explained to her. "I felt terrible about not being in it. And, with my guitar back, I'll be able to perform what I originally was going to! Thank you so much Ginger! You're the best friend any Elf has ever had," Elfis told her, and had to look away quickly so she couldn't see his eyes watering when he said it.

Ginger smiled, "No problem, E," she assured him.

"Well," Elfis said after he had composed himself, "We've got some practicing to do today!"

Ginger laughed. "I thought I was supposed to take a break, and find a balance?"

"Easy for you," Elfis countered. "You're going to win this thing hands down, but if I want to come in second, I need to practice, I haven't played for an entire week after all!" The two friends laughed.

"What's so funny?" Kris asked the two of them. He had just arrived to check his time slot when he spotted his two friends.

"What's up, Kris?" Elfis said, giving his new friend a high five. "You all ready for tonight?"

"I hope so, although I don't know why I even entered, Ginger's going to win obviously," Kris said good naturedly.

"Shut up you two," Ginger said, but couldn't completely get rid of the smile on her face.

Elfis then told Kris about what Ginger had done, and halfway through the story Kris's face cracked into a huge smile and Elfis paused. "What are you smiling at?"

Before Kris could respond Ginger cut in. "Signing you up was Kris's idea."

Elfis couldn't quite conceal the shock that must have shown on his face.

"That's right," Ginger responded to the look. "The two of us were talking about how much of a shame it would be if you actually didn't perform, and Kris said we should sign you up!"

Elfis was in awe, and he surprised both himself and Kris by wrapping him up in a big bear hug as well. "Thank you, Kris, that means a lot!"

"Don't mention it," Kris responded coolly.

No one spoke for a minute, and then Elfis broke the silence, "Well, we've got some preparation to do, let's get out of here." All three elves laughed as they walked away from the school.

The three elves parted ways and agreed to meet back up before the talent show to walk to school. Elfis went inside and saw both of his parents in the living room enjoying their day off. "Mom, Dad, guess what?" Elfis asked them.

"What?" they responded simultaneously.

"I'm in the talent show tonight!" Elfis blurted out. "Ginger signed me up without telling me, and now I'm performing!"

"That's great news. That Ginger, she's just the best," Holly said fondly.

"What are you going to do son?" Elfis's father asked him.

"Well..." Elfis hesitated. "I was thinking about playing the guitar."

"The guitar huh?" his father questioned and paused. "I think that's a great idea," he finished, and Elfis let out a relieved sigh.

"Thanks Dad! Well, I'm going to go practice." Elfis ran up the stairs and grabbed his guitar.

Elfis sat on his bed and started to figure out which songs he was going to play. He decided he would play three songs. He was going to open with Heartbreak Hotel, then Jailhouse Rock, and finally, he would conclude with Hound Dog, naturally. Satisfied with his idea, he started practicing. He knew all the songs already, but if he wanted to impress people tonight, he needed them to be perfect. He wanted to win of course, but the talent show was about more for him than just winning.

This was the first time he was going to play in front of a big crowd. He wasn't breaking any rules, he wasn't going to have to turn down his music, and no one was going to interrupt. For Elfis, this was the first of what he hoped was going to be dozens, if not hundreds, of concerts that he would perform. So, while winning would be great, there was more at stake for Elfis tonight than maybe anyone else could possibly realize.

Elfis set about practicing, and after an hour or two he was feeling really confident about his chances tonight. He assumed Ginger would win, and he also thought she deserved to, but he did hope to take second place, and thought that maybe he actually had a chance at doing that.

Elfis was just about to run through his set one more time, when he was interrupted by his dad. "What in the North Pole is going on up here!" His dad burst into his room angrily.

"Nothing," Elfis said defensively, "I'm just practicing for tonight, you said it was a good idea."

"Well, not like that, it isn't. Your mother and I have been listening to this racket for the last two hours and I can't believe what I am hearing."

Elfis was confused, nervous, and angry, all at the same time. His father said the guitar was a good idea, even encouraged Elfis to play it, and after everything they talked about yesterday, Elfis couldn't understand this reaction from his father. "What do you mean?" Elfis was gearing up for another argument. Had his dad gone out of his mind?

"You're never going to win the talent show with those three songs!" And just as Elfis was getting ready for another shouting match with his father, Jack's face broke into a smile.

"Well, what do you think I should play?" Elfis earnestly asked his father.

"Son, we both know you can play Elvis's entire catalogue from memory. But this is a talent show, and just copying the King's songs doesn't demonstrate what you can do." Elfis looked up at his father, not quite comprehending what he was talking about.

"So, I shouldn't play Elvis?"

"You're going to perform three songs, right?" Jack asked rhetorically. "Why don't you play two Elvis songs, and then one Elfis song. Show everyone there tonight what you're capable of: play an original, Elfis composition!"

"But my songs aren't even close to as good as Elvis's. What if no one likes what I play?" Elfis asked.

"Well, if you want to be a rockstar, now is the time to start. Unless you want to move to Las Vegas you won't become a musician just playing Elvis hits," Jack said to his son. "You've got to try, Elfis, and if people don't like your music that's okay. You keep working and you keep practicing, and maybe one day you'll have a selection of hits that rivals the King's."

Elfis listened to his father. It was weird taking musical advice from a man who only yesterday Elfis thought hated music, but not only was it good advice, it was nice to hear it from his father. "Thanks Dad, maybe I will throw in an Elfis original tonight!"

"Well, whatever you decide, your mother and I can't wait to hear you play tonight!" Jack assured his son.

Chapter 14

The Talent Show

Elfis spent the entire afternoon practicing, and as the talent show crept closer the butterflies in his stomach started flapping harder and harder. Before Elfis felt even remotely prepared, Frost poked his head into Graceland.

"Time to go superstar," Frost said to his brother. Elfis looked up and Frost saw the color drain from his face. "What's wrong, E?"

Elfis swallowed and let out a huge sigh. "What if I mess up tonight?" he asked his brother.

"What?" Frost asked. "I've heard you play the guitar a million times; you're going to be great!" he reassured his brother.

"But I've never played in front of this many people. I've never played in front of anyone really," Elfis said, and Frost heard the panic in his voice.

"Well, that's not entirely true." Elfis looked up at his brother skeptically. "You played for dozens of elves in the factory not so long ago," Frost said and winked at his brother.

Elfis let out a weak chuckle. "That was a little different, I was just goofing around."

Frost looked down at his brother with a smile. "How is this any different? Just get on the stage and goof around a bit, have fun! And, if you get really nervous, just look at the first row. That's where we'll all be sitting. Just block everyone else in the auditorium out and focus on us. You've played for us a hundred times, right?"

"Yeah, I guess so," Elfis answered his brother.

"So, just do it one more time. You're going to be great, and, on the very off chance you mess up, we'll be there for you after the show all the same," Frost finished, and he wrapped Elfis in a big hug.

"Thanks Frost," Elfis said, and hugged his brother back. The color had started to return to his face, and the butterflies hadn't gone away, but Elfis thought maybe they were starting to get tired and go to sleep for the night.

"You've got this," Frost said. "Now let's go, we don't want to be late."

"I'll meet you downstairs," Elfis told his brother, "I need two minutes to change."

Elfis walked downstairs and saw his mom, dad, brother, and sister, dressed and waiting for him. All four of them gasped when they first saw the hopeful rock star. Elfis had changed from what he was wearing into a purple homage to Elvis. He had a bright purple jacket on that matched his pants perfectly. The suit was complemented with a huge belt three times as wide as any belt that had ever existed before it, with an even bigger purple belt buckle that had stars going around the outside. Elfis had also taken it upon himself to glue or sew dozens of fake gold stars and shapes onto his jacket. His pants came down and flared out at the bottom to all but cover his shoes, and his hair was styled and slicked back. He had also popped the collar on his purple jacket and had his guitar resting on his back and strapped around his chest. "Well," he tentatively asked his family. "What do you think?"

All at once the four of them started talking over each other, telling Elfis how good he looked. "This is amazing," his father said laughing, "you look just like Elvis! They should hang a picture of you in Graceland."

"Where did you get this?" his mother asked, smiling, and in absolute shock.

"I've been working on it for a while now, Ginger and I made it," Elfis said, delighted by his family's response.

"You look great, dude," Frost said to him.

Elfis looked down and saw his sister trying to pull one of the stars off of his jacket. "Stop it," he said to her and picked her up.

"Can you make me one, Elfis?" his sister asked him.

"Does that mean you like it?" Twinkle nodded at her brother. "Then of course I'll make you one," Elfis assured his sister. "Well, let's get out of here, I've got a talent show to win."

The five of them made their way to the school. They caught Ginger and her parents as they were leaving their house as well. Ginger screamed when she saw Elfis. "Oh my god, you look amazing!" she said. "I can't believe it!"

Elfis's parents greeted Ginger's and the four of them fell behind to catch up and talk. Frost, Twinkle, Ginger, and Elfis walked a bit ahead of them, as Ginger continued to talk about Elfis's costume.

"Hey Ginger," Frost said to Elfis's best friend.

"Oh," Ginger said shyly. "Hi Frost, you look great." As she said that Ginger's eyes popped open, and she wished more than anything that she could take those words back.

She looked down embarrassed. Elfis smiled. Ginger was never shy or embarrassed around anyone, but no matter how many times she denied it, she had a huge crush on Frost.

Frost smiled at her reassuringly. "Thanks, are you all ready for tonight? What are you doing up there?"

Ginger managed to stammer out, "It's a surprise."

"Well, I can't wait to see it."

Before Ginger could respond, and to save her from any further embarrassment in front of his brother, Elfis cut in. "There's Kris, let's go catch up with him, Ginger. We'll see you after the show," Elfis said to his brother.

"Good luck you two," Frost said to them as they sped up ahead.

Elfis nudged Ginger. "Real smooth back there," he gently teased her.

"Oh, shut up," Ginger said, and nudged him back with a smile. The two elves caught up with Kris, and the three of them walked towards the school. When they got to the auditorium, they saw chaos in front of them. Hundreds of elves were wandering around with no real rhyme or reason. Elf parents were catching up with elves they hadn't seen, and a low rumble filled the auditorium as two hundred different conversations took place simultaneously.

Elfis, Ginger, and Kris tried to make their way towards the back, jostling and bumping elves out of their way. They made apologies as they went, but no one even acknowledged or felt the young elves, there was too much going on. As they finally got backstage, they saw dozens of elves nervously trying to squeeze in an extra minute or two of practice before the talent show started. The three friends found a corner to wait in and just a few minutes later they heard the noise start to die down on the other side of the curtain. Just then the lights went out, and all talking abruptly halted. Mr. Blizzard's voice boomed out as he spoke into the microphone. "Good evening, ladies and gentlemen, and thank you all so much for joining us here tonight for the three hundredth annual talent show. We have twenty-four elves backstage who have been working tirelessly to prepare their talent and give you all a great show." The elves backstage heard a polite applause as Mr. Blizzard said this. Mr. Blizzard continued his introduction, but Elfis had stopped listening, he was starting to feel those butterflies wake up in his stomach, and as he looked around, he saw the familiar faces of his classmates all displaying some signs of nerves and anxiety. "And remember, the elves will each have a maximum of ten minutes to perform. When they hear the bell—" Mr. Blizzard rang a small bell to demonstrate the sound. "—They have to stop." Mr. Blizzard finished his speech and the audience applauded once more.

"And now, without further ado," Mr. Blizzard said, and the students could hear the excitement in his voice, "allow me to introduce Bubbles!" The audience clapped enthusiastically, and Bubbles, a classmate of Elfis's, let out a huge sigh and walked out on stage.

As the evening progressed, the students backstage waited impatiently for Mr. Blizzard to call their names so they could perform. There had been several big reactions from the audience, and the talent show was off to a great start. The three friends didn't talk much to each other as they waited. Finally, Mr. Blizzard called for Kris to go perform. Ginger and Elfis each gave him a high five, and he walked out on stage.

Ten minutes later, they heard Mr. Blizzard ring the bell, and an applause from the audience. At this point there were only about ten elves left backstage. A few more elves were called to perform, and then finally Mr. Blizzard called for Ginger. She stood up and bumped fists with Elfis.

Ginger's time started and Elfis watched her from backstage. He had never seen her work so quickly or efficiently. From the second the clock started to the instant before the bell rang, Ginger worked feverishly. She darted around the stage attaching reindeer limbs to reindeer bodies and nailing together wood for Santa's sleigh. When the bell finally did ring, Ginger had put together a perfect replica of the sleigh and had managed to build six reindeer as well! Mr. Blizzard asked her to place her toy on the display table, and when the audience saw it actually worked electronically, they erupted into applause. Elfis was clapping from backstage along with the rest of the crowd. He knew Ginger was an exceptional toymaker, but he couldn't believe she had done all of that in only ten minutes. He looked at his best friend standing up on stage. She looked a little disheveled, and completely exhausted, but she was beaming at the reaction from the audience.

As Ginger left the stage to join the crowd, Elfis sat back down. It seemed almost a guarantee that Ginger would win. Elfis was still shocked by how well her model had turned out, and he was thrilled for his friend. Now he just had to get through his time slot, and this would all be over.

Elfis continued to wait for his turn while the last few elves were introduced to perform. Finally, it was only him backstage and as if from down a tunnel he heard Mr. Blizzard announce his name. "And finally tonight, last, but certainly not least, he was a last minute entry, please welcome Elfis!" The audience clapped politely, as Elfis slowly walked to the center of the stage. He moved the display table out of his way, and as he did, he heard hushed voices commenting on his outfit, and the guitar strung across his back. He was, after all, the only elf that was not making a toy, and the audience seemed as confused at this fact, as they did about his outfit.

Elfis finished clearing the stage and he looked out at the hundreds of people all staring up at him. He thought to himself what would they do if he turned around and walked backstage? As he was thinking about this, he looked at the front row, and saw not only his family, but Ginger, looking up at him. Elfis locked eyes with his brother, who gave him a thumbs up, and then took a deep breath.

Elfis started to play and as soon as he played the first chord all of his nerves and anxiety disappeared. Elfis started his set with the Jailhouse Rock, and by the end of the song, he heard some elves clapping along to the beat of his playing. He felt incredible – he was actually playing a live concert. He had wanted this for his entire life, and he couldn't believe it was finally happening. The song ended, and Elfis immediately started to play Hound Dog. When the audience heard this song start, some of the more audacious members of the crowd actually stood up and started dancing.

Elfis finished and the crowd burst into a round of applause. Elfis had about four minutes left of his allotted time, and for one second, he considered stopping. But, as the audience started to quiet down, he thought about what his father had said, that he would never be a rockstar if he didn't play his own music. As the audience settled back, looking up in anticipation, Elfis decided that moment to play one of his songs.

Elfis had been working on this song for months, but he

had never played it for anyone before, not even Ginger. Taking one more deep breath before he did it, Elfis started to play. From the first chord he played, the audience loved it. Elfis had written a song that somehow combined elements of Christmas music with that of Elvis's carefree and aloof style of rock and roll. By the end of his song the entire audience was up out of their seats, dancing and cheering.

Finally, Elfis wrapped up his set, and the auditorium erupted! As he looked out at the reaction of the crowd Elfis thought two things. One was that maybe he could actually be a rockstar, maybe he had a chance to leave his mark on music. And two, even if he didn't make it as a musician, this was one of the best nights of his life. He had performed an actual concert, in front of actual people, and they had enjoyed every second of it.

As the crowd settled back into their seats, Elfis went to join his family and Mr. Blizzard came back out on stage. "Wow, that was really something," he said to the audience. "What a night this has been. Before the winner is announced, I just want to thank all of our students for their participation, and I think they all deserve one more round of applause for all the hard work and time they put into their performances." The audience heartily agreed with Mr. Blizzard and cheered for everyone one more time. "And now," Mr. Blizzard interjected, "here to announce the winner, please give a hand to Mrs. Claus!" There was another round of clapping as Mrs. Claus came out on stage.

"Thank you, Mr. Blizzard, for that warm welcome," Mrs. Claus said as she got to the microphone. "And thank you to each and every elf that performed tonight. You all did such a wonderful job!" she said to the students. Elfis and Ginger looked at each other. They had no idea Mrs.

Claus actually announced the winner herself. The two waited on tenterhooks as Mrs. Claus continued to talk. She thanked the audience for their patience and for coming to the show, and she once again explained the prize. Finally, after what felt like an eternity, Mrs. Claus had finished talking and was looking out at an expectant audience.

"I am delighted to announce that for the first time in three hundred years of watching and judging this pageant, we have a tie for first place." The audience was absolutely silent. "So please, join me if you will, in congratulating both Ginger Tinsel and Elfis Sparkle, as they have become the first joint champions in talent show history."

There was a brief moment of silence as the audience processed this piece of information, and then Kris started clapping, and was followed by several hundred elves clapping and cheering for the two winners as they walked up on stage absolutely stunned. The two best friends went up to shake hands with the most important woman in the North Pole, in a state of utter disbelief. Mrs. Claus beamed down at them, and she winked at Elfis. "That was quite a performance," she said to him over the roar of the crowd. "And you, Ms. Ginger." Ginger looked up at Mrs. Claus terrified. "I know who I'm going to come find next time we have trouble with Mr. Claus's sleigh."

"Thank you, ma'am," the two elves said simultaneously, as the audience continued their thunderous applause.

Epilogue

Elfis woke up the next morning and had to ask his brother to make sure he hadn't dreamed the night before. Frost reassured him that he had in fact won the talent show along with Ginger, and Elfis still had trouble believing it. He went downstairs to have breakfast with his family and all of them were still talking about the talent show.

"So, when are you going to cash in on your trip in Santa's sleigh?" Elfis's father asked him at the table.

"I'm not sure," Elfis replied. "We'll have to find a time that works for both of us, and obviously we need to make sure that works for Santa, but I would like to go soon. I still can't believe I actually won!"

"Well," said Jack as he looked down at his son, "you're not going to be able to go on Saturday mornings for a while, so you'll need to take that into consideration."

Elfis looked up at his father confused. "What do you mean? Why not?" he asked.

"Well, I guess you could go on a Saturday morning, but that's the only time your new guitar teacher can give you lessons, so you'd have to skip your new class, but that's up to you, I guess." Jack looked down at his son smiling.

Elfis looked up at his father, processing what he had just been told. "Are you serious?"

Jack continued smiling down at his son. "There's no point denying it after last night – you're a rockstar, why try and fight it?"

Elfis stood up so quickly he knocked over his chair, as he ran to hug his father. "Thanks Dad," he said as his father hugged him back, "for everything!"

The End